Holme Lee

The Life and Death of Jeanne d'Arc

Called the maid V.2

Holme Lee

The Life and Death of Jeanne d'Arc
Called the maid V.2

ISBN/EAN: 9783337299507

Printed in Europe, USA, Canada, Australia, Japan

Cover: Foto ©Raphael Reischuk / pixelio.de

More available books at **www.hansebooks.com**

THE LIFE AND DEATH

OF

JEANNE D'ARC,

CALLED *THE MAID.*

BY

HARRIET PARR,

AUTHOR OF "IN THE SILVER AGE," ETC.

"The nobleness of life depends on its consistency,—clearness of purpose,—quiet and ceaseless energy."
JOHN RUSKIN—*Ethics of the Dust.*

IN TWO VOLUMES.

VOL. II.

LONDON:
SMITH, ELDER & CO., 65 CORNHILL.
1866.

" Man, when he resteth and assureth himselfe, upon divine Protection, and Favour, gathereth a Force and Faith; which Humane Nature, in it selfe, could not obtaine."

LORD BACON—*Essayes of Atheisme.*

CONTENTS.

I.

THE BUYING AND SELLING OF THE MAID.

IT would be but to make a choice amongst the vices to say where lies the blackest shame of Jeanne d'Arc's cruel tragedy— with Charles VII., who abandoned her; with the Duke of Burgundy and Jean of Luxembourg, who sold her; with the English council, who delivered her up to the Church; or with her ecclesiastical judges, who condemned her. One thing, however, stands for true—princes of her own nation betrayed her to death; and priests of her own nation accomplished her death. Of the English lords on whom recoiled the deep dishonour of it, the English sage might have been speaking when he said, "How oft the sight of means to do ill-deeds makes ill-deeds done!"

In the cabals of the University of Paris was promptly and authoritatively marked out the road by which to bring the Maid to her desired end, and

amongst the great lights of the University were
found men of craft and skill enough to travel over
all its obstacles with the air of doing a pious duty.
Jeanne was captured on the 23d of May; on the
25th, news of the event reached the capital; on the
26th, the clerk of the University wrote to the Duke
of Burgundy, in the name and under the seal of
Martin Billormi, vicar-general of the Inquisition in
France, requiring that she should be forthwith
delivered up to the Holy Office, as vehemently
suspected of divers crimes savouring of heresy.   It
was common fame, he said, that in many cities and
places of that kingdom, she had sown, dogmatised,
and published errors, from which had arisen great
breaches and scandals against the honour of God
and the faith, to the perdition of many simple
Christians; which things neither could nor ought
to be passed over without suitable reparation.   The
University, in its own name, addressed an equally
urgent exhortation to the noble Catholic prince,
admonishing him of his duty to maintain the faith
in its purity, and to aid the Church in taking away
her enemies.

The Duke of Burgundy vouchsafed no answer
to these demands.   The Maid was worth a king's
ransom at least, and that neither the Inquisition
nor the University was likely to pay.   Perhaps,
also, he felt indignant at the first blush of the
request, that he would give her up to be burned.

He had his honour to look to. She was a person of such high chivalry, that there was no knight in Christendom whose fame overshadowed hers. By all the ordinary courtesies of war, she was entitled to the privileges of a prisoner of war. She had been a generous foe, if a resolute and successful foe. Neither cruelty nor treachery could be laid to her charge. Her life was pure ; her brief career most glorious. To him, personally, she had appealed as a prince of France, to make peace with France ; and throughout his alliance with England, he had never forgotten that he was a prince of France, and that it was an alien race he had helped to her throne. The inevitable tendency of events was now towards the restoration of Charles. It might be soon, or it might be late, but it would come. To sacrifice the heroine who had given events this forward impetus, might put a new difficulty between himself and the king. He did nothing, therefore ; and Jean of Luxembourg, whose prisoner the Maid more immediately was, frankly refused to give up his prize, unless well paid for her.

Had Charles intervened at this moment, perhaps he might have bought her, if the regent had not come forward to outbid him. But Charles was absolutely quiescent. There is no discoverable trace that he ever spoke a word, lifted a finger, stirred a foot to save her. Nor does it appear that

the English council felt any great alacrity to possess her, so long as she was believed to be safe in
the prisons of Burgundy.   Neither did the Inquisition show any stomach for the prosecution the University sought to thrust upon it.   One of its own
officials, the Inquisitor of Toulouse, had concurred
with numerous dignified clergy of Charles's side in
pronouncing the Maid a good Catholic and good
Christian ; and the Holy Office was *one*, whatever
party prejudices and party hatreds divided the
churchmen of France.   If, therefore, she was to be
the sacrifice of these prejudices and hatreds, some
more active and interested agent must be sought
than the Dominican friars, servants of the court of
Rome.

The University had such an agent ready to hand
in Pierre Cauchon, the fugitive Bishop of Beauvais,
a member of the English council, and the conser-
vator of its own privileges.   Jeanne d' Arc had
been captured in his diocese, and he was put forward to claim her as her Ordinary.   By dint of
contemplating the revenge proposed through his
means, the regent acquired a longing for it ; the
Cardinal of Winchester, too.   The prelate offered
them his powerful aid.   Able, well-reputed, artful,
ambitious, he was the very man to glide into
the unjust judge, and to work iniquity for any
great reward.   And the archiepiscopal see of
Rouen was vacant.   Who more fit to fill it than
Pierre Cauchon ? the splendid scholar, the mag-

nificent priest, strong in the friendship of Burgundy. His animosities were as poignant as those of his accomplices. They were moved by wicked policy to defame Charles as having prevailed through the magical arts of a witch—and so was he; by malignant spite to be avenged on a woman who had humbled their pride to the dust—and so was he; by cruel rage and fear to be rid of the mysterious influence that paralysed the arm and cowed the spirit of the bravest amongst their soldiers—and so was he. They worked together like one mind, and saved appearances admirably, the University of Paris suggesting, urging, and cordially approving all they did. The extreme adherents of the Burgundian faction were, indeed, thoroughly de-nationalised; and thus it came to pass that they could clamour and scheme to compass the death of the Maid who had begun the redemption of their country; and to satiate their own malice, could make themselves the avengers of the foreign enemy whom she had checked in enslaving it.

Nearly two months, however, elapsed before the English council were brought to move in the matter. It was their policy to keep in custody their most redoubtable French prisoners; and perhaps distrustful of Burgundy's power to resist the temptation of a great ransom, supposing Charles able to give it, they at length consented

to buy her out of his hands; and prepared to
levy the money by a tax on Normandy. Pierre
Cauchon undertook to deal with the duke, and
bestirred himself with the more energy because
there was a rumour afloat that some friends of
the Maid were planning her rescue. On the 24th
of July, he arrived in the camp before Compiègne, which still held its besiegers at bay, accompanied by an apostolical notary, and an envoy
from the University of Paris, bringing letters to
Burgundy and his nephew. In the name of Henry
VI., the bishop presented to them a schedule of
summons, requiring, as Ordinary of the diocese in
which the Maid had been taken, that she should
be surrendered to him. The schedule ran thus :—

"This is what the Bishop of Beauvais demands
of the Lord Duke of Burgundy, the Lord John of
Luxembourg, and the Bastard of Wendonne, on
the part of our lord the king, and on his own part
as Bishop of Beauvais.

"That the woman who is commonly called Jeanne
the Maid, prisoner, be sent to the king to be delivered to the Church to take her trial, because she
is suspected and accused of having committed
many crimes, such as sorceries, idolatries, invoca-
tions of demons, and many other things touching
our faith and against it. And although it seems
that she ought not, considering this, to be regarded

as prize of war ; nevertheless, for the remuneration of those who took and have kept her, the king will liberally give to them the sum of six thousand francs, and to the Bastard who captured her, he will assign a pension of two or three hundred livres.

"*Item*, And the bishop requires, on the part of the king, of each and all of the above-named, that the woman, having been taken in his diocese, and under his spiritual jurisdiction, shall be surrendered to him, to take her trial, as to him belongs. To which he is ready to listen, with the assistance of the inquisitor of the faith ; and if need be, with the assistance of doctors in theology and canon-law, and other notable persons, expert in matters of jurisprudence, as the case shall require, that it may be wisely, piously, and maturely done, to the exaltation of the faith, and the instruction of many who have been deceived or misled on account of this woman.

" *Item*, And in conclusion, if in the manner aforesaid, all or any of the above are not content to comply with this requisition ; although the capture of this woman be not like the capture of a king, prince, or other person of great estate, [yet if it chanced that such were taken, whether king, dauphin, or other prince, the king might have him, if he would, on giving to his captor ten thousand francs, according to the law, usage, and custom of France,] the bishop summons and requires those

by name above-mentioned, that they deliver the
Maid to him, on his giving surety for the said sum
of ten thousand francs: and the bishop, on the
part of the king, according to the form and penalties
of the law, demands that she be given and surrendered to him as above."

When Pierre Cauchon presented this curious
schedule to the Duke of Burgundy, there were in
his company a crowd of nobles and gentlemen.
When the duke had read it, he handed it to his
chancellor, Nicole Rolin, and told him to pass it
to Jean of Luxembourg.   When he also had read
it, the envoy from the University delivered his letters.   Burgundy and his nephew received and
perused them—long letters to the same purpose
as the bishop's schedule, but more pious in phra-
seology, and more venomous in spirit.

" The University of Paris to the illustrious prince,
the Lord Duke of Burgundy.

"Very high and mighty prince, our dread and
honoured lord, we recommend ourselves humbly to
your highness.

"Although we have before written to your highness, humbly beseeching you that the woman called
the Maid, being, by God's mercy, in your subjection, should be put into the hands of the justice of
the Church, duly to take her trial for the idolatries

and other matters touching our holy faith, and the scandals which, by her means, have come on this kingdom, together with the mischiefs and innumerable inconveniences that have arisen therefrom, we have had no answer, and know not whether any fit provision has been made to inquire into the case of this woman. But we fear much, lest, by the lies and seductions of the devil, and by the malice and subtlety of wicked persons, your enemies and adversaries, who are, as we hear, striving their utmost to deliver her, she should be taken out of your subjection in such a manner as God will not permit; for, verily, in the judgment of all good Catholics understanding it, so great a wrong to the holy faith, so enormous a peril, disadvantage, and injury to the people of this kingdom, has not happened within the memory of man, as it would be, if she escaped by such damnable ways without making suitable reparation. And it would be greatly to the prejudice of your honour and to the Christian name of the House of France, of which you and your noble progenitors have been and are the chief members and protectors. FOR THESE CAUSES, our very dread and honoured lord, we humbly supplicate you anew, in favour of the faith of our Saviour, for the maintenance of His holy Church and His divine honour, and also for the good of this very Christian kingdom, that it will please your highness to put this woman into the hands of the inquisitor of the faith, and to send her to him securely, as we besought you before; or else that you will give her, or cause her to be given, to the reverend father in God, the Lord Bishop of Beauvais, in whose spiritual jurisdiction she was apprehended, that he may make her trial in the faith, as to him appertains by right, to the glory of God, to the exaltation of the said holy faith, and to the profit of good and loyal Catholics, and also to the honour and praise of your royal highness, whom may our Saviour keep in prosperity, and finally bring to His glory."

The letter of the University to Jean of Luxembourg was equally imperative, and could leave him in no uncertainty as to what would be the ultimate fate of his prisoner if he complied with its requisition.

"*The University of Paris to the noble and powerful knight the Lord John of Luxembourg.*

"Very noble, honoured, and powerful lord, we recommend ourselves very affectionately to your high nobility.

"Your noble prudence understands well that all good Catholic knights ought first to employ their might and power in the service of God, and afterwards for the public good. The first oath of the order of chivalry is to guard and defend the honour of God, the Catholic faith, and holy Church. You remembered this oath well when you employed your noble powers and personal efforts in apprehending that woman who calls herself *the Maid;* by whom the honour of God has been beyond measure affronted, the faith excessively wounded, and the Church very deeply dishonoured, and through whose means idolatries, errors, bad doctrines, and other inestimable evils and inconveniences have come upon this kingdom. And, verily, all loyal Christians ought to thank you for having done so great a service to our holy faith and to all this kingdom ; and as for us, we thank God and your noble prowess with all our hearts fervently.

" But it would be a small thing to have taken her if there did not ensue the reparation that belongs to the offences perpetrated by this woman against our mild Creator, His faith and Church, with her other innumerable misdeeds. It would be a greater wrong than before, a worse error would abide with the people, and an intolerable offence would be offered to the Divine majesty if the matter rested where it is, or if it happened that this woman were delivered or lost—as it is said some of our adversaries are labouring to deliver her by wily ways, and what is even worse, by ransom. But we hope God will not permit so great an injury to come upon His people, and also that your good and noble prudence will not suffer it, but will know how to pro-

vide against it ; for if thus an escape were made for
her, without due reparation, it would be to the irre-
trievable dishonour of your nobility, and of all those
who had concerned themselves in it.   And because,
in such scandals, delay is very perilous and prejudicial to the kingdom, we pray you very humbly,
and with cordial affection to your powerful and
honoured nobility, that in favour of the Divine
honour, for the preservation of the holy Catholic
faith, and for the good and exaltation of all this
kingdom, you will deliver this woman to justice,
and will send her to the inquisitor of the faith, who
has peremptorily requested and demanded it, that
he may make inquiry into her great charges, so that
God may be pleased, and the people edified in good
and holy doctrine ; or else, that you will surrender
her to the reverend father in God, our very honoured lord, the Bishop of Beauvais, who also has
demanded it, she having been apprehended in his
diocese.

"These two, the prelate and inquisitor, are her
judges in the matter of the faith ; and all Christians,
of whatsoever condition they be, are bound to obey
them in the present case, by the penalties of the
law, which are heavy. In doing so, you will acquire
the grace and love of God ; you will be the means
of exalting our holy faith, and also of increasing the
glory of your very high and noble name, and even
that of the very high and very mighty prince, our

dread lord and yours, the Duke of Burgundy. And every one will be bound to pray God for the prosperity of your very noble person, whom, may our Saviour guide by His grace in all things, and finally reward with His eternal joy."

Neither the ferocious, impatient zeal of the University, nor the requisition of the Bishop of Beauvais, with the offer of a royal ransom for the Maid, were sufficient to move Burgundy and his nephew to immediate compliance with their demands. A bargain of such momentous importance could not be concluded in haste. The pious doctors of Paris, nurtured on the aliment that had formed the mind and conscience of Jean Petit, would have made a short end of her, if she had been flung to them, and the Inquisition, of whose name they made such free use, could have been set in motion. What cause delayed the decision of the duke and his kinsman does not appear. The formal menaces of the king, the Church, and the law, were mere smoke as addressed to them—they might very safely defy them all. Neither does it appear what were the wily efforts, alluded to by the University, making amongst the Maid's party for her deliverance. No city—not even Orleans—claims the modest honour of having offered to pay, or help to pay, her ransom. There is no memorial that any of the great princes and lords, her companions-in-arms, ever made one effort to rescue her by force.   Charles's panegyrists and apologists can claim nothing for him on her account, can put in no plea, but that when she was dead, he grieved for her.   Scruples of honour might possibly weigh with Burgundy and Luxembourg ; but from the final conclusion of the barter and sale of the Maid, it is more probable that they had not yet been offered their price.   But, however it was, the Bishop of Beauvais and the envoy of the University went their way back to Paris, with their mission for the present unachieved.

Jeanne d'Arc was still at Beaulieu when Pierre Cauchon paid his visit to the camp before Compiègne.   No doubt his errand came to her knowledge ; for she made an attempt to escape—a futile attempt—and she was soon after removed to a greater distance from the scene of the war.   Her new prison was the castle of Beaurevoir, near Saint-Quintin, where the wife of Jean of Luxembourg and his aged aunt, the Countess of Ligny and Saint-Pol, resided.   Jean d'Aulon had ceased to attend her now ; but the two ladies used her with the kindness and consideration all good women had for her at all times.

Jeanne's treatment in the prisons of Burgundy was not harsh ; but, as she refused to give her faith not to try another escape, she was consigned to an apartment in the donjon at Beaurevoir, and was

strictly guarded day and night. She had, however, liberty to go out for air on the top of the tower,
which was of a great height, and commanded an
immense prospect over the plains of Picardy.

It was only the beginning of August, but already
captivity pressed cruelly on her. Many a bright
harvest day must she have sat watching over the
long brown levels for the friends that never, never
came. She might pray to die ; but hope of deliverance rose above the wish for death. Ah ! if she
were at Chinon, and Charles at Beaurevoir, would
not she have come thundering at its gates to release
him ? Her flight without farewell might seem un-
kind, but he knew her necessity; it could not—it
could not have made him forget all she had done
for him and for France ! Surely he would bring
or send her help ! Surely he would not abandon
her to her enemies quite ! Or if he did, would not
the people strike a blow for her ? Would not
Orleans and Tours and Blois remember the day
of their peril, and succour her in hers ? Would not
Alençon—would not La Hire, Dunois, or Saintrailles try to lead a rescue for her ?

It was a blessed thing for Jeanne she did not
possess those gifts of universal prescience and divination that her adorers once sought to credit her
with ; for if she had possessed them, she would
have seen only enemies chaffering over the price
of her blood, the king folding his hands in peace

and quietness, his ministers busy blackening her name, a few poor priests and people praying for her, and the common crowd of citizens and soldiers going all their own way, on their own business, with never a thought or a care beyond it.

Both the Countess of Ligny and the Lady of Beaurevoir stood Jeanne's friends to the utmost of their power. They besought that she might not be given up to the English; and Jean of Luxembourg · seemed to listen to their entreaties with favour. Then they tried to put Jeanne herself into the way of propitiating her adversaries. Her fighting days were over. Her male habit now no longer disguised the feminine beauty of her form, and they were extremely anxious that she should exchange it for her natural dress. They offered her fit clothing, or materials to make it in any fashion she preferred, but she refused to accept either.

"I would do it to please you rather than any ladies in France, except my queen ; but I have not yet my Lord's leave," said she. Jeanne did not think her fighting days over, if others did.

Now and then, to divert her melancholy, Haimond de Macy, a young gentleman in the train of Jean of Luxembourg, was sent to visit her in his name, and to entertain her with gay and cheerful conversation. He saw her what she always was—modest and quiet, and not unsociable ; but when he grew familiar, and attempted to carry on his mission with such freedom as might be, perhaps, the best love-making manner of a Burgundian soldier, he found himself repulsed with the liveliest indignation. But he bore her the better respect for it, and was quite sure that her martyrdom was her entrance into paradise.

The old Countess of Ligny died, and Jeanne lost a safeguard. Her days at Beaurevoir were very weariful, but they were pleasant days in comparison with what were to follow. At Beaulieu, Jean d'Aulon had brought her news of events that were happening outside her prison; news oftenest of the hard siege Compiègne was still bearing up against long after she had seen the last harvest-sheaf carried from the fields. But each time he spoke of it, his tidings were more hopeless, and one day he had said despondently, "That poor city of Compiègne that you have loved so much will, by now, have been put into the hands of the enemies of France."

"Nay, it never will be," Jeanne had replied. "None of the places that the King of Heaven reduced and restored to the obedience of the gentle King Charles by means of me, will be retaken by his enemies, if he be but diligent to keep them."

But worse intelligence arrived now. Compiègne seemed nearing its extremity, and the besiegers had sworn, when they took it, to put to the sword every man and woman within its walls, and every child over seven years of age. Jeanne, when she

heard that, thought it would be happier to die than
to live.

"Oh, will God thus suffer to perish all those good
people who have been so loyal to their king!" cried
she; and fell to reasoning with herself on the
mysterious ways of Providence, her *voices* answering her now encouragingly and hopefully, now with
remonstrance, now with reproach, as the thoughts
of her heart swayed to and fro between trust and
despair.

She besieged Heaven with prayers for the city,
and for herself, that she might escape to its succour. It was nearly the end of September then,
and one afternoon she heard that the Bishop of
Beauvais had arrived at Beaurevoir. The price for
which the Duke of Burgundy and Jean of Luxembourg would sell her had been hit upon at last.
Burgundy wanted the quiet acquiescence of the
regent while he defrauded his aunt Margaret of
Brabant, Brussels, and Louvain; Jean of Luxembourg wanted the quiet acquiescence of his kinsman and liege lord, Burgundy, while he appro-
priated the estates of Ligny and Saint-Pol, to the
prejudice of his elder brother. There was the ten
thousand francs' ransom for them to share besides,
after giving his little portion to the Bastard of Wendonne; and if they felt the need of it, there was
the decent cover-all offered them by the University,
to disguise their unknightly treason as a bounden

duty to God and the Church. The bishop's ne-
gotiation seemed likely to prosper, and it was
whispered to Jeanne that she was sold, and was
about to be given up to her adversaries.

"Oh, I would rather *die* than be given up to the
English!" was her agonised response. "I would
rather die than fall into the hands of the English!"

In her grief and terror, she flew up the tower and
out upon the roof, thinking, Oh, how should she
escape her foes! Would not God aid her to escape,
and go to the relief of those poor beleaguered
people in Compiègne? Her *voices* answered her,
*Be patient; God can help Compiègne, and He will
help it.* If God will help Compiègne, oh, will He
not deliver me? *Be patient; thou canst not be delivered until thou hast seen the king of the English.*
I would never see him of my own good will; oh,
let me escape. *No; be patient.* Oh, my God, save
me! St. Katherine, St. Margaret, behold my need!
My burthen is greater than I can bear! *God will
help thee.* But now, *now*—it must be now! and with
a wild, passionate appeal to Him, she sprang from
the top of the tower.

She was taken up like one dead; those who
found her thought she was dead. When she began
to return to herself, they told her she had fallen
from the tower. In her moanings and sobbings of
pain, they could hear her praying to die, rather

than be given up to the English. She had no
broken bones or other serious injury, beyond the
shock ; but for several days she refused to eat or
drink. Despair almost had hold of her, but all her
thoughts were aspirations to God ; and presently
the spark of hope that never quite goes out but
with the breath of life, quickened again into a
flickering light, and the cloud passed from heart
and brain. She heard her *voices* bidding her confess her sin, and she obeyed.

" I have done wickedly. Pardon me, O my God,
and comfort me !"

And the sense of Divine mercy and pity did comfort her, and her *voices* whispered that she was forgiven in Heaven. She bore a long, heavy penance
of pain, but·she never lacked soothing in it.

The Bishop of Beauvais left Beaurevoir as he had
left Compiègne—with nothing finally settled. Jean
of Luxembourg could not yet quite make up his
mind. His wife besought him to turn his back on
the temptations with which he was tempted. But
presently intervened his brother Louis, another
reverend father in the Church, the Bishop of Thourenne, the Chancellor of France for the King of
England, and proposed to transact the horrible piece
of traffic for him.

A great and unexpected event had happened. The
siege of Compiègne had been raised.

It was raised late in October. The inhabitants had been then four months without selling bread in public, and were reduced to utter famine. Burgundy and the English had completely compassed the town with trenches and towers, and had occupied and stopped every approach. It was with the utmost difficulty that the inhabitants could send out a messenger to carry news of their destitution to the Count of Vendôme, the chief in command of the Beauvoisis. But as soon as he heard of their danger, he assembled about a hundred and fifty lances, got supplies of food together, and accompanied by Marshal de Boussac and Saintrailles, marched down between the river Oise and the forest of Cuise towards Compiègne, hoping to throw in relief, but hoping nothing more ; for the enemy were in very strong force all about it.

A rumour had, however, been noised in the camp of the allies that Vendôme was followed by a powerful army, and the English and Burgundians drew out for battle. Guillaume de Flavy and the people of the town perceived that nothing but a sudden and desperate effort could save them. They sallied out, women as well as men, and attacked a fort on the road to Saint-Lazare, about a bowshot and a half from the city, in which had been left a garrison of three hundred soldiers. After being twice repulsed, they carried it by storm, and thus opened a way for those bringing succour. Vendôme entered

the town without losing a man, while the English
and Burgundians were holding themselves in reserve
against his imaginary host. It did not appear that
day; and the next, to the astonishment of the besieged, the enemy drew off two separate ways, leaving the garrisons in the towers to shift for themselves,
and abandoning in their sudden departure great
spoils of war. The people of Compiègne rallied
from their surprise, and took possession of all. The
fortresses were surrendered and dismantled, and before the end of the month Guillaume de Flavy and
Saintrailles were scouring the open country to clear
it of their enemies.

Great was the rage of the English and false French
in Paris at this ignominious conclusion to their long
and costly siege. The panic and flight had been
as inexplicable and precipitate as if the Witch-Maid
of the Armagnacs had reappeared amongst them in
her first force. The English believed their arms
would never prosper while she lived ; and they
dreaded lest this reverse of theirs, and the deliverance of Compiègne, news of which would rejoice
her heart in her prison, might restore the confidence
of Charles and his party in her, and inspirit them to
undertake some grand expedition to recover her
mighty aid. The Bishop of Beauvais and the Bishop
of Thourenne went to work once more. Burgundy
and Jean of Luxembourg shut their eyes, and tried
not to see the Judas-work they were doing. The

blood-money was counted out to those who had it; and the Maid, bought and sold at last, was carried from Beaurevoir to Arras—one stage forward on her journey to Rouen, the scene of her martyrdom.

No sooner was the bargain concluded than the University of Paris, with jubilant servility, wrote to congratulate the poor little nine-year-old king, Henry VI., on having got secure possession of the terrible scourge of the English after so many delays. Thus ran the letter :—

> " *To the very excellent prince, the King of France and England, our very dread and sovereign lord and father.*

" Very excellent prince, our very dread and sovereign lord and father, we have heard news that the woman called *the Maid* has now been put into your power, of which we are very joyful; trusting that by your sound ordinance she will be brought to justice, to repair the great iniquities and scandals notoriously come on this kingdom, through her means, to the great prejudice of the Divine honour, of our holy faith, and of all your good people.

" And because it belongs to us especially, according to our profession, to extirpate such manifest iniquities when our Catholic faith is touched, we cannot dissimulate the long delay of justice in the case of this woman, which must have displeased every good Christian, and your royal majesty more than any other, from the great obligations you owe to God, in recognition of the high gifts, honours, and dignities which He has conferred on your excellence. And though we have before several times written, and now again write on this matter, very dread and sovereign lord and father, always offering our humble and loyal recommendations that there may be no negligence in dealing with it, we humbly pray, for the honour of our Saviour Jesus Christ, that your high excellence will be pleased to command this woman to be put speedily into the hands of the justice of the Church—that is to say, the reverend father in God, our honoured lord the Bishop of Beauvais, and also the inquisitor ordained in France, to whom especially belongs the cognisance of her misdeeds in what touches our holy faith ; to the end that due inquiry may be made into the charges against her, and such reparation as the case demands, for guarding the holy truth of our faith, and putting all false error and scandalous opinion out of the thoughts of your good, loyal, and Christian people.

"And it seems to us very proper, if it be the pleasure of your highness, that this woman should be brought into this city to have her trial made publicly and surely ; because masters, doctors, and other notable persons being assembled here in great numbers, the discussion of her case would have a wider reputation than elsewhere; and it is also fit that her reparation should be made in this place, where her doings have been divulged, and have become excessively notorious. And in doing this, your royal majesty will testify great loyalty to the Sovereign and Divine Majesty; and may He grant to your excellence continual prosperity and bliss without end.

"Written at Paris, in our solemn general congregation, celebrated at Saint-Maturin, the xxi. day of November, the year MCCCCXXX. Your very humble and devout daughter, the University of Paris."

It was winter, leafless, bleak winter, on the plains of Artois, when Jeanne d'Arc was carried from Beaurevoir to Arras, and from Arras to the castle of Crotoy, a dreary fortress at the mouth of the river Somme, held by an English garrison. On her way thither, her escort rested with her one night at the castle of Drugy, close by the town and abbey of Saint-Requier. Two of the old monks, Jean Chapellin, the almoner, and Nicholas Bourdon, the provost, with some of the principal townsfolk, went to pay her a visit of respect, and all were touched with compassion for her great adversity and her persecuted innocence.

At the castle of Crotoy there happened to be another prisoner when Jeanne arrived—Nicolas de Guenville, chancellor of the cathedral-church .at

Amiens. Jeanne was allowed to attend mass daily, said by him in the chapel; to him she confessed, and from his hands she received the Eucharist for the last time, until the morning of her martyrdom.

At Crotoy, too, she saw the last kind faces of women, and heard the last words of love and tenderness that ever she was to hear in this world. Several ladies of Abbeville, matrons and maidens, came five leagues by boat down the Somme to see her, as "a marvel of her sex, and a generous soul whom God had inspired for the good of France." Jeanne thanked them for their charitable visit, and at parting kissed them all, bidding them pray for her. They went away weeping, and saying one to another, how constant she was, and how resigned to the will of God, all whose blessings and consolations they devoutly wished might rest upon her.

It was the beginning of December when the English guard that was to convey the Maid to Rouen arrived at Crotoy, and received her into their custody. They carried her in a boat across the mouth of the river to Saint-Valéry; the cold winter wind setting in from the sea. How did its gray, limitless tumult touch her? Did her *voices* whisper courage and comfort louder than the waves wailed sorrow?

From Saint-Valéry Jeanne was taken to the castle of Eu, and thence to Dieppe. From Dieppe, a little before Christmas, she was brought to

Rouen, and lodged in the castle, in the great tower.

The English court was in the Norman capital when she arrived there—the king residing in a fine palace, still unfinished, the building of which had been begun by his father, Henry V.

II.

THE PRELIMINARIES OF THE TRIAL.

EAN D'AULON parted with the Maid at Beaulieu. He had never left her for a day after Charles VII. intrusted her to his care until she was carried to Beaurevoir. Writing of her five and twenty years after her death, to Jouvenal des Ursins, the then Archbishop of Rheims, who had appealed to him for information concerning her, as the person who had perhaps known her more intimately than any other, he says:—"She was a young girl, beautiful and well formed, . . . a very devout creature. I firmly believe, her deeds and noble behaviour considered, that she must have been inspired, and guided by our Lord. . . . Never, during all the time I was in her company, did I see or know anything of her save what was good. . . . She loved all a good Christian ought to love, and especially she loved a true good man whom she knew to be of chaste life." . . .

Pierre Cusquel, an inquisitive citizen of Rouen, who obtained admittance to Jeanne's prison soon after her coming, by interest with the master-mason of the castle, saw her in the middle chamber of the great tower, to which he mounted from the court-yard by eight steps. It was a large room, and had a light looking towards the fields. He was told that she had been kept in an iron cage, made to hold her in an erect position, confined by the neck, wrists, and ancles, when she was first brought to Rouen. She was then chained by the feet to a ponderous log of wood. Waking, she was always ironed to this log of wood : sleeping, she was ironed by the legs with two pairs of heavy fetters locked to her bed. She lay down to rest in prison clothed as she lay down when on the march with the army ; but instead of that brave gentleman D'Aulon to watch her, she had three English guards, servants of John Grey, a royal equerry, who was appointed her chief keeper. Besides these three shut in with her at night, two others kept the door outside.

Jeanne d'Arc was more than five months in Rouen castle. The Earl of Warwick, governor of the young king, a hard, inflexible man, had over-sight of the prison arrangements. Beyond the rigorous restraint which he and the Bishop of Beauvais ordered as necessary to Jeanne's safe custody, (for she openly avowed her determination

to escape if she could,) her usage was not, at first,
grossly bad. The Duchess of Bedford, a good
woman, certified to the bishop, on the authority of
several notable matrons of Rouen, whom she sent
to visit her, that she was a pure and perfect
maiden ; and the duchess herself laid a charge
upon her guards to treat her with respect. A little
later, when Jeanne complained of the violence of
two of these men, and expressed her terror of
them, the Earl of Warwick reprimanded them
severely, and dismissed them from their office.
But she never ceased to dread her English keepers,
and the inhumanities in which they were permitted,
and perhaps encouraged, after a while, justified all
her distrust.

Her greatest privation was, that from the time
of her arrival at Rouen, she was laid practically
under the ban of excommunication. She was
neither suffered to hear mass, nor to receive the
sacrament of the altar. She was even denied confession. Inexorably cut off from all those outward
solaces of religion by which she set such store, her
thoughts reached out with perpetual longing to
Heaven. Her hallucinations returned vividly as
at Domremy. Pure in heart, all her visions were
good, all beautiful, all divinely consolatory. The
echo of her supplications thrilled with the full
assurance of love, and peace, and happiness eternal.
The trumpet-tongue of St. Michael was silent after

she left Crotoy, but the voice of the Comforter
pierced the walls of her prison; morning, noon,
and night, in the sweet church bells of Rouen,
St. Katherine and St. Margaret talked with her as
friend with friend.

When the exalted moments passed, she did not
sink into base dejection. Her spirit was long in
breaking. To her judges she showed as intrepid a
countenance as ever she had shown to her enemies
in the field. She felt the bad atmosphere of their
malice, hatred, and revenge pressing all round her,
and she stood valiantly on her own defence; upheld
to the very last by the expectation that she should
be delivered out of their hands with triumph.

The Duchess of Bedford, like the ladies at Beaurevoir, tried to prevail on her to resume the dress of
her sex, and even caused a tailor, named Simon, to
make her a petticoat, and to carry it to her in her
prison. The man had been bidden to employ per-
suasion, argument, and possibly some gentle force
to induce her to accept it; for when she refused, he
put his hand softly on her bosom as if to unloose her
jacket. But the Maid's powerful young arm was
free, and indignant at his presumption, she dealt
him a slap in the face, which caused him to rue it.
The tailor's misadventure became soon one of the
many bits of gossip that were circulated cautiously
in Rouen concerning the famous prisoner at the
castle.

There was a great diversity of feeling about her
in the city, but it was necessary to take heed of expressing any feeling in her favour ; for the regent's
power was arbitrary, and when the justice of the
Church laid hold on a victim, woe betide the man
who ventured to impugn her motives or her tender
mercies! Though all Normandy was English, there
existed a leaven of old loyalty amongst the people ;
and whoever in Rouen chafed under the foreign yoke,
and had heard the truth of the Maid's exploits,
had a shrewd suspicion that it was far more from
hatred to Charles VII., and from revenge and malice
against his victorious champion, than from zeal to
the faith, that her trial was begun with an ostenta-
tious carefulness, publicity, and cost which defied
and challenged the observation of all the world.

The regent and the Cardinal of Winchester were
men to go leisurely about their work, and to make
it sure.   Where would be the profit of instructing a
prosecution against the Maid if it were to be interrupted ?   And Charles, if he would, might arrest it
at any stage, by appealing to have her removed to
Rome, or to Bâle, where was about to meet a General
Council of the Church.   Georges de la Trémouille
was a traitor to Jeanne ; the Archbishop of Rheims
was no better.   Before a step was taken towards her
trial, her adversaries were probably well certified
that it would be suffered to run its course without
let or hindrance—not necessarily certified by any

understanding with Charles's government, but by its complete inaction. Seven months had elapsed since the University first agitated the proceedings to be taken against her, and no remonstrance or opposition had come from the clergy of the French party. Jean de Gerson, a man to have stood by his original opinion of the Maid, was dead. But the Archbishop of Rheims, the chief judicial and ecclesiastical functionary of the kingdom, who had presided over the jury of churchmen at Poitiers, and, as their mouthpiece, had pronounced favourably of her, had notoriously changed his views when he gave out that pride went before her fall, and that for her disobedience God had forsaken her. It must have become widely known that the faith of her party had declined, even if it had not been reversed. The University groaned over the slowness of the English government, embarrassed by scruples, hesitations, and doubts of success. It had no drag on its own pious hatreds. Aware of its weight as a spiritual body, it apprehended no resistance from its political adversaries, and tried to push on the trial with indecent haste. It even took to task its own admirable representative, the Bishop of Beauvais, for not using more diligence in the affair; and when it wrote to congratulate the little king on having got possession of the Maid, it wrote to the prelate also, admonishing him that if he had done his endeavours, she would have been long before in the hands of the justice of the Church, and her case well advanced.

At last, on the 3d of January 1431, the English council brought its lingering deliberations to a close, and, in the name of the king, granted an act making over the Maid to the bishop for trial. It was explicitly stated in this document that if she were cleared of the charges brought against her for the faith, she would still remain the prisoner of the English. The enormous ransom they had paid for her, entitled them to keep her; and that she might be kept securely, though by law and reason she ought to have been removed into the ecclesiastical prison, when she became the object of an ecclesiastical prosecution, she was left at the castle in custody of her English guards.

The royal mandate issued for Jeanne d'Arc's trial ran, in substance, as follows :—

"Henry, by the grace of God King of France and England, to all who shall see these present letters, greeting.

"It is sufficiently notorious how, sometime ago, a woman who caused herself to be called Jeanne *the Maid*, forsaking the habit and vesture of the feminine sex, did, against the Divine law, . . . clothe and arm herself in the fashion . . . of a man ; did do and commit cruel acts of homicide, . . . and gave the simple people to understand

that she was sent from God, and had a knowledge
of His Divine secrets ; together with many other
perilous doctrines, very prejudicial and scandalous
to our holy Catholic faith. In pursuing these deceits, and exercising hostility against us, . . . she
was taken armed before Compiègne, . . . and
has since been brought prisoner to us. And because she is by many reputed as guilty of divers
superstitions, false teachings, and other treasons
against the Divine Majesty, we have been earnestly
required by the reverend father in God, our friend
and faithful counsellor, the Bishop of Beauvais,
. . . and also exhorted by our very dear and
well-beloved daughter, the University of Paris, to
surrender her . . . to the said reverend father in
God, that he may proceed against her according to
the rule and ordinance of the divine and canon laws.
Therefore is it that we, in reverence and honour for
the name of God, and for the defence and exaltation of the holy Church and Catholic faith, do devoutly comply with the requisition of the reverend
father in God, and the exhortation of the doctors
and masters of . . . the University of Paris, and
ordain that the said Jeanne shall be delivered by
our officers who have her in their charge to the
reverend father, . . . whenever and as often as
shall seem to him good, that she may be interrogated, examined, and her trial made. . . . And
we hereby command our officers to give her to him

without denial, . . . as they are by him required.
We also command our judges, and subjects, French
and English, that to the reverend father, . . . and
to all others who shall be ordered to assist . . .
the trial, that they . . . give them no hindrance,
. . . but if they are required . . . that they
give them care, help, defence, protection, and comfort, on pain of severe punishment.   Nevertheless,
it is our intention, if the said Jeanne be not convicted nor attainted of the crimes above-named, nor
of any of them, nor of others concerning our holy
faith, to have her and take her again to ourselves.
In witness of which, we have affixed our common
seal, in the absence of the great, at this present.
Given at Rouen, the third day of January, in the
year of grace MCCCCXXX. and of our reign the ix.
On the part of the KING, by his Great Council."

There is no mention in the royal act of any demand for the Maid's trial by the Inquisition.   Indeed, the Holy Office manifested an extraordinary
reluctance to be drawn into the affair.   Jean
Graverent, the grand-inquisitor for France, when
invited to join the Bishop of Beauvais as judge, excused himself on the plea of business elsewhere.
His vicar for the diocese of Rouen, Jean Lemaitre,
was equally anxious to evade the responsibility.
The preliminaries of the trial did not arrange themselves so swiftly or smoothly as Jeanne's adversaries

desired ; but the bishop, who had undertaken to make it, and to make it, as he said, "*a beautiful trial,*" was bold and adroit.   He was sure of the strong support of the University to the end of his labours; and by means of its members, he was able to constitute a tribunal of so imposing a presence, that if the Inquisition should persist in refusing him its countenance, he would still offer a front of learned and pious authority to the world, capable of averting any charge of malpractice.

The prelate had the lure of a magnificent fee in prospect.   The English court being in Rouen, it was resolved to try Jeanne there rather than in Paris.   Driven from Beauvais, Pierre Cauchon had neither territory nor clergy of his own ; but the chapter of Rouen cathedral granted him letters to act in that diocese as ecclesiastical judge ; and the privy council of Henry VI. sent a recommendation under their seal to the Pope for his translation to the vacant see.

The 9th of January was the first day of this famous cause.   The bishop convoked a meeting of doctors and masters in the king's council-house near the castle, to hear the official report that had been drawn up about the Maid, and to appoint the persons who were to serve on her trial.   To this meeting came Gilles de Ruremont, Lord Abbot of Feçamp, a member of the royal council; the Abbot of Jumièges, the Prior of Longueville-Gifford, and

Nicolas Venderez, the bishop's chaplain. Raoul Roussel, the treasurer, and Nicolas Loiselleur, Nicole Coppequesne, and Robert Barbier, canons of the cathedral of Rouen, were also present.

To the office of promoter and proctor-general in the cause was nominated the bishop's fellow-fugitive, Jean d'Estivet, canon of Beauvais and Bayeux, a base man, brutal in language and behaviour, who was called in derision *Benedicite*. Jean Delafontaine, master of arts and licentiate in canon-law, was constituted counsellor, commissioner, and examiner in ordinary. Two notaries of the archiepiscopal court of Rouen, Guillaume Manchon and Guillaume Colles, called *Boisguillaume*, priests, were deputed to act as clerks; and Jean Massieu, priest and rural dean, as usher of the court, to execute the mandates of the judge. Their letters of institution were drawn up and granted forthwith.

Four days later, there was a meeting at the bishop's house to hear read certain informations that had been collected about the Maid, with notes of events concerning her that were common fame. Monks and other stealthy emissaries had been, for some time past, travelling hither and thither in the bishop's service gathering these informations; following her footsteps from childhood to the hour she left her father's house; thence to Chinon, to Orleans, to Rheims, to Paris; back beyond the Loire to Saint-Pierre-le-Moustier and La Charité;

then from Sully to Lagny, and to and fro, through
her last campaign, up to the moment of her capture, and beyond it to Beaulieu and Beaurevoir.
What would not serve the purpose of the prosecution was set aside ; and the rest of the informations
it was decided to cast into articles, to see whether
there was matter enough whereon to base an accusation for offences against the faith. Ten days
later the same court assembled again in the same
place to deliberate on the articles thus composed.
It was agreed that they contained grounds on
which to interrogate the prisoner. The informations themselves were never communicated in their
original form to any of the assessors besides who
sat on the trial ; but the substance of them appeared in the Act of Accusation drawn up at the
close of the Maid's public and private examinations.
It was then manifest that in her brightest days
Jeanne had traitors near her, and in her confidence ; that there were miscreants wherever she was
known, ready to lie about her, to give a malevolent
turn to her most innocent acts, to charge upon her
as crimes the honours accorded to her by the king,
and the love of the poor, adoring people who alone
were faithful to her memory.

Meanwhile, a royal messenger had been despatched
to Paris to summon six distinguished doctors and
masters of the University to assist the bishop as
special counsellors. They were chosen with much

discrimination ; were all apparently moderate men, and not one, whatever his feelings, was apt to betray them by violence of manner. Three—Jean Beaupère, Pierre Morrice, and Thomas de Courcelles—had just been elected deputies from the University to the Council of Bâle. The others were Nicole Midi, a noted preacher, Jacques Texier, a learned and gentle Franciscan, and Girard Feuillet. Of the six, Thomas de Courcelles was at once the youngest, of the highest reputation, and the greatest hopes. He was only nine-and-twenty ; but he was already spoken of as Gerson's successor ; and he became, in the sequel, the most renowned scholar of the University, and the triumphant champion of the liberties of the Gallican Church. He was an austere, eloquent man, naturally timid and modest ; and him the Bishop of Beauvais set very forward in the business of the trial. Whether his respect for the prelate, who was a great canon-lawyer as well as a great divine, made him a dupe, or whether he put aside his principles out of complacency, it is certain that he did many things in it that troubled the conscience of his maturer age, and that were a deep stain on a character otherwise noble and honourable. He and all the Paris counsellors shared the bishop's political prejudices ; all helped him zealously in his work, and were well paid for it by the English government. Two doctors of medicine—Jacques Tiphaine and Guillaume de la

Chambre—whom the judge likewise summoned from the capital to assist him, came with less alacrity than the theologians; they thought it strange they should be called on a trial for the faith, and pleaded that it was not in their way; but on a second bidding they went to Rouen, and stayed there until the cause was concluded. The Maid's sanity might possibly be revoked in doubt, and the bishop thus provided against the contingency.

On the 13th of February, the six counsellors and the officials previously appointed, met at the bishop's house, and in the presence of Venderez, Loiselleur, and Coppequesne, were each and all required to make oath that they would faithfully exercise the trust reposed in them. There was then held a consultation, as a result of which, the bishop addressed a formal requisition to the vicar of the inquisitor at Rouen to sit with him as judge on the great trial about to open. Jean Lemaitre presented himself before the assembly, bringing his letters of vicarship, and on the ground that his powers did not extend to a trial belonging to the diocese of Beauvais, he declined to act unless furnished with a special commission by his superior. The bishop therefore despatched a letter to the grand inquisitor, representing how important was the cause, and urgently requesting him either to come to Rouen himself, or to send his vicar powers to officiate in his stead. The prelate designed to achieve the Maid's destruction with all the pomp and circumstance, with all the solemnity and rigorous observance of external rule usual in trials for the faith. It would not have answered the purposes of her adversaries, either English or Burgundians, that the thing should be done in a corner, as a thing they were ashamed of doing. All Christendom had heard of her marvellous deeds : let all Christendom hear of her terrible retribution! To clothe the matter with the utmost order and legality, it needed no more, after the accession of the Paris counsellors, than the presence of a judge of the Holy Office. Jean Lemaitre consented to appear in the court as an assessor, awaiting the grand inquisitor's answer to the bishop, and it was then determined to proceed to business forthwith. On the 20th, citations were distributed to the ecclesiastics of Rouen, and a citation was the same day carried by Jean Massieu to the prisoner, requiring her, under pain of excommunication, to appear on the morrow, at eight o'clock in the morning, before the court appointed to try her for the heresies and other crimes of which she was accused and defamed.

Massieu was a good and tender-hearted man. His conduct to Jeanne d'Arc was distinguished by kindness, pity, and respect from first to last. He read the mandate to her in her prison. She replied that she would willingly obey it, but bade him go to the bishop, and in her name, require that he would convoke for her trial as many ecclesiastics adhering to the French king as to the English. She also humbly supplicated that before she was brought into the presence of her judges, she might be allowed to hear mass.

Both requisition and prayer were denied.

III.

THE SIX PUBLIC SESSIONS OF THE TRIAL.

The First Session.

ON Wednesday, February 21, at eight o'clock in the morning, the Bishop of Beauvais and the court before whom the Maid was to be tried, met in the chapel of Rouen castle. There sat on the tribunal as counsellors or assessors at the opening of the cause, fifteen doctors of divinity, four doctors of canon law, seven bachelors of divinity, twelve bachelors of canon law, and four licentiates of civil law—forty-two ecclesiastics, of whom all but eight belonged to the body of secular clergy. The regulars were the abbots of Feçamp, Jumièges, Cormeilles, and Saint-Katherine-du-Mont, the priors of Longueville-Gifford, and of the Dominican convent at Rouen, Jacques Texier, a Franciscan, and Jean Lefèvre, an Augustine monk.

The business of the court began by the reading

of the king's letter surrendering the Maid to the Bishop of Beauvais, and the letter of the chapter of Rouen cathedral authorising him to act in that diocese. The prosecutor, Jean d'Estivet, then read the citation of the judge addressed to the prisoner, and his citation to the clergy. Then followed Massieu's relation of their presentment, containing Jeanne's demand for assessors of the French party, and her petition to hear mass. The promoter required that she should appear at once before the tribunal as it was then constituted. The bishop consented, and while Massieu went to bring her from her prison, the bishop informed the court that, following the counsel of certain of the learned doctors and masters, leave to hear Divine service had been refused her, because of the iniquities with which she stood charged, and because of her persistence in wearing the immodest habit of a man. Her just requisition for assessors of her own party was entirely passed over, and she did not repeat it.

While the bishop was still speaking of her prayer to hear mass, Jeanne was led into the chapel by Massieu, and conducted to her place in front of the tribunal—John Grey, William Talbot, and John Berwick, three of her guards, following. Her chains had been taken off, and she appeared to the crowd of counsellors and spectators who thronged every corner of the chapel, a girl evidently very young, but with an air of perfect dignity and self-possession.

She had her hair still cut round, and she wore the ordinary dress of men ; "no sign of her sex appearing, except that form which nature had put upon her." All her armour in which she delighted had been taken away, and all her bright bravery besides, down to her *Jhesus Maria* ring, and the garb in which she presented herself before her judges was black.

As soon as she had taken her place, and the rumour that ensued at her entrance had ceased, the bishop began to expound to her, that having been captured in his diocese, and her deeds in breach of the faith being common fame throughout France, the king had given her up to him to make her trial according to law and reason.

"Wherefore Jeanne," continued he, in the serious sweet tone of a benevolent judge, "desiring, in this trial, with the gracious assistance of Jesus Christ, whose cause is in question, to fulfil the duty of my office for the preservation and exaltation of the faith, I earnestly warn and require you, that for the speedy despatch of the present business, and for the relief of your own conscience, you will speak the full truth concerning those things of which you are accused respecting the faith."

She was then bidden to take her oath on the Gospels to speak the truth. Jeanne was utterly ignorant of law and judicial forms. She had no conception whatever, for a long time, that her trial

tended to her death. But the dulcet manner of
the bishop was incapable of hiding his malevolent
disposition towards her. She knew him already as
the negotiator of her purchase. He was one of
those the secret thoughts of whose hearts she penetrated with the subtle glance of intuition; and to his
command that she would take the customary oath,
she replied, "I do not know upon what you wish to
question me. Perhaps you may ask me such things
as I shall not be able to answer."

The bishop replied, "You must swear to speak
the truth on all that shall be asked you concerning
the faith."

"I am unlearned; will you give me no counsel
to help me to answer?"

"You must answer for yourself; no counsel can
be given you."

"I will swear to tell you the truth of my father
and mother, and of what I have done since I came
into France; but of the revelations made to me on
the part of God, never have I told them to any
one, unless it be to my king; nor will I tell them,
though I should have my head cut off, because I
have had warning by my *counsel* to show them to
no other. A week hence, however, I shall know if
I ought to reveal them to you."

There was so much murmuring and noise amongst
the audience the moment Jeanne mentioned her
revelations, that the notaries complained they could

not hear what she said, and much was lost, and escaped record. The bishop reiterated that she must swear to tell the truth on all matters touching her faith; and at length she knelt down, laid her hands on the Gospels, and swore in that form, omitting to add her former reservation.

Jeanne, in the presence of her judges, though fearless and often defiant, was no longer the frank and simple girl she had appeared before the friendly doctors at Poitiers. It was her endeavour, from the beginning of her trial, to lay herself as little open to her enemies as she could, and when the peril of her situation dawned upon her, it developed all her latent intellectual *finesse*.

The bishop opened the interrogatory by asking her what was her name.

" In my own country I was called Joanneta; since I came into France, I have been called Jeanne."

She was then questioned of her parents, of her birthplace and baptism, of her godfathers and god-mothers, and was asked her age. She said she believed she was nearly nineteen. Being interrogated of her religious training, she replied, " My mother taught me *Pater Noster*, *Ave Maria*, and *Credo*. I never learnt anything of my faith but from her."

"Since you know the *Pater Noster*, recite it before us," said the bishop.

"Hear me in confession, and I will recite it gladly."
The bishop was not moved by this touching offer of

her confidence. He declined to hear her in confession; *that* would have deprived him of the satisfaction of acting as her judge, but he renewed his
command, that she should repeat the prayer.
Jeanne was firm : " I will not repeat it, unless you
hear me in confession."

" We will grant you one or two notable ecclesiastics of your own party, before whom to say it,"
proposed the judge.

" Neither will I say it to them, unless they hear
me in confession," was her response.

The bishop had no design of affording her that
relief for the heart-ache. He ceased from questioning her; but before giving her her dismissal
for the day, he solemnly prohibited her from
escaping out of the prison assigned her in Rouen
castle, under pain of being declared convicted of
the crime of heresy.

" I do not accept that prohibition," said she ; " so
that if I do escape, no one can blame me for having
broken faith, for I have never given it to any person." She then complained of being fettered, to
which the bishop answered, that she had several
times endeavoured to escape, and therefore she had
been ordered to be kept in chains, that she might
be kept more safely and securely.

" It is true that I wished, and always shall wish
to escape," said she ; " as it is lawful for all prisoners to do."

At this hearing, the bishop called on John Grey, John Berwick, and William Talbot, her guards, to swear upon the Gospels that they would keep her strictly, and that they would permit no one to have speech or sight of her without a licence from him. This done, Jeanne was appointed to appear again before the court at eight o'clock the next morning, and was then conducted back to her prison as she had been brought from it.

Amongst the very few persons who had obtained permission to see Jeanne d'Arc, before the opening of her trial, was a magistrate of Rouen, Pierre d'Aron, who went in company with Pierre Manuel, an advocate of the king's court. There were several English guards present, and she was chained as usual. The halo of her glory did not shine in her prison, and her visitors had no delicacy in asking her any questions their curiosity prompted, or in making any jest their dulness was equal to. Such intrusions must have been insufferably odious to her ; but in the evening, after her first public examination, she had a great and unexpected delight. Her guards suffered to enter a stranger, who told her he was a friend from her own country, from the marches of Lorraine, and that he was, like herself, a prisoner for the cause of Charles VII. She was left with him alone, by a stretch of charity on the part of her guards, which might have

warned her that all was not right. But she suspected no treachery. She only thought that here
was a man who could tell her how her king's affairs
were going—who could talk to her of Domremy,
and of all the pleasant places that she loved. The
stranger was, in fact, the bishop's familiar and spy,
Nicolas Loiselleur, a canon of Rouen cathedral.
The practice of the Inquisition, which the judge
aspired to follow with marked scrupulosity, permitted the introduction of a false confidant to an accused person, and he had availed himself of the ex-
pedient, in the hope of surprising from Jeanne some
details which no lips but her own could furnish.

When Loiselleur was admitted into her presence,
the prelate and the Earl of Warwick, with the two notaries, Manchon and Boisguillaume, entered a room
adjoining the prison, where every word she uttered
was audible through a hole purposely contrived in
the partition-wall. Manchon, who had the instincts
of an upright man, and the will to be honest, objected
to this method of obtaining information against the
prisoner. The bishop said Jeanne spoke admirably of her revelations, and that he wanted to hear
her speak of them without reserve. They listened,
and Manchon recognised Loiselleur's voice in
earnest conversation with her. The spy soon found
the key to unlock Jeanne's heart, and she poured
out before him her memories of her village, of her
home and friends—talked of the Oak-wood, the

Beautiful May, and the meadows, of the fountain, and the happy fête-days of her childhood. Then he insidiously drew her on to speak of her visions and *voices*—their coming and going, their promises, and the work they had set her on doing. While she, all unsuspicious, was confiding to him her halluci-nations, and their overpowering influence on her, the bishop bade the notaries write down what she said. Manchon refused; if she repeated the same things in court, he would register them, but he would register nothing in this surreptitious manner. Loiselleur cautioned her against betraying any of her secret *counsel* to her judges,—assured her they could do her no harm, and encouraged her with such a fair show of sympathy and sincerity, that when he left her, she believed that she had found one, in the midst of her enemies, who would be a faithful adviser, and true friend.

To have seen a kind face where yet she had seen only faces full of hatred, mockery, or cold curiosity: to have heard a kind voice where she yet had heard only voices of admonition, menace, insult, ridicule: what a revival of hope and courage must they have brought her! Loiselleur was a supple and skilful traitor; and as a priest, the easier to disguise. He had to appear amongst the assessors in the court, and he had, by and by, to enact the part of her *director* in his natural character; but she never re-cognised him as the feigned friend from her own country, who had been admitted to her at the beginning of her trial, by the apparent kind connivance of her guards. He was a man his fellows did not like, but he was not ashamed of his spy's work; for he even jested about it, in talking to Thomas de Courcelles.

There were some very lax consciences amongst the counsellors. Many suspected, and some knew for a certainty, that a false confidant had been given to the unhappy prisoner whom they were trying for her life; and all who knew Loiselleur were well assured that such a confidant was purposely given to mislead, and not to guide aright. But never one interfered to save her from betrayal. Their silent acquiescence in this, as in other nefarious deceits and traps, which the forms of the inquisitorial law served perfectly to conceal—not only from the outside world, but also from the less learned or less experienced assessors—made some of the great doctors whom the bishop had called to his tribunal, no better than his accomplices in the judicial murder he had undertaken to do.

The Second Session.

The tumult in the chapel the previous day had determined the bishop to hold the future public sessions of his court in a small hall, adjoining the great hall of the castle; and that the examinations might be carried on without interruption, two English guards were placed at the door, with orders to exclude all who had not a permission from him to enter. The lay authorities of the government, with the single exception of the Earl of Warwick, kept themselves entirely in the background throughout the trial; but some great lords of the court were always present amongst the audience, and two or three English secretaries who made notes for the council and the king.

In crossing the castle-yard from the prison tower to the great hall, Jeanne d'Arc had to pass with her guards in front of the chapel. As Massieu was conducting her to the tribunal, she begged him to let her pause a minute or two before the door to pray. He would not have dared to let her enter, but he granted this poor little petition, and when she had made her brief supplications, he brought her forward to the place where the court was sitting.

The consistory was fuller than on the first day, seven more ecclesiastics having received a citation from the bishop; and amongst them a physician of Rouen, Guillaume Desjardins. Loiselleur did not appear, and Manchon, when he discovered his absence, conjectured that he was concealed in a great curtained window, where were ensconced the English secretaries, and others, making garbled notes for the judge.

The legalised notaries had their places below

the tribunal, at a table where sat the Paris counsellor, Jean Beaupère, to whom the bishop had
entrusted the task of conducting the public interrogatories. Beaupère had his own clerk, Jean
Monnet, and opposite to him was placed the Maid.
She was permitted to sit; for the court, which
opened at eight o'clock, did not rise until eleven,
and she was under examination the whole of the
time.

The bishop began with an admonition to Jeanne
to take her oath simply and absolutely to tell the
truth.

"I swore yesterday—that ought to suffice you.
You burthen me too much," replied she. After
some difficulty she took the oath, but *now* she an-
nexed to it the reservation she had omitted before.

Jean Beaupère, a shrewd, dry doctor of fifty,
who was to lead Jeanne's examination, had already
formed his theory about her. Combining his personal observation with the articles and memoranda
furnished to him, he had come to the conclusion
that she was not corrupt, but that she was subtle
with all the subtlety of woman. Her visions and
voices, he believed to be not supernatural, but
traceable, in part, to physical causes, and in part
to imagination and human invention. He began
his interrogatory with a short exhortation to her to
be sincere, and to answer as she had sworn.

Jeanne reminded him of her reservation, saying :

"You may ask me some things about which I could tell you the truth, and others about which I could not tell it. If you were well-informed about me, you ought to wish me out of your hands. I have done nothing save by revelation."

Beaupère inquired what age she was when she left home, and on her declining to tell him, he asked if she had, in her youth, learnt any occupation.

"Yes; I learnt to sew and to spin. I should fear no woman in Rouen at sewing and spinning. And at home with my father and mother, I took charge of the household work."

"Of the performance of your religious duties—did you attend confession?"

"I confessed to my own priest, and when he was absent, to some other, by his leave. Once or twice also, I confessed to mendicant friars—that was at Neufchâteau. And I received the sacrament of the Eucharist at Easter."

The examiner now asked her abruptly about those *voices* she had, which she said were *voices* from God. Jeanne refused to answer—this question was an approach to her revelations. She was urged, argued with, threatened, and finally she confessed to them, saying, "I was about thirteen when I had a *voice* from God, to help me to rule myself. The first time I heard it, I was very much afraid. It was in my father's garden at noon, in the summer."

"Was it on a fast-day?"

"I had fasted the day before. The *voice* came from the right-hand, by the church, and there was a great light with it. When I came into France, I heard it frequently." Beaupère wished to learn a little more about it before her coming into France, and in reply to his further questions, she said, "If I was in a wood, I heard the *voice* coming to me. It was a good *voice*, and I believe it was sent me from God. After I had heard it three times, I knew it was the *voice* of an angel. It has always kept me well, and I understand perfectly what it says."

"Did the *voice* give you any instruction for the welfare of your soul?"

"It bade me be good, and go to church often; and it told me that I must go into France."

"In what shape did that *voice* appear to you?"

"I shall not tell you. Two or three times a week it said that I must go into France, until I could no longer rest where I was. It told me I should raise the siege of Orleans, and that Robert de Baudricourt would give me people to conduct me. Twice he repulsed me; but the third time he received me, and sped me on my way, appointing me a knight, an esquire, and four servants for company. He made them swear to take me safely; and when I left him, he said, 'Go! and let what will come of it, come!'"

" By whose advice did you assume your male habit ? "

Jeanne's assumption and persistence in retaining this dress had been marked as one of her most abominable offences. She first refused to answer the question at all ; and when it was insisted on, she gave various replies, the sum of which was that the blame of it she did not charge on any man. Jean de Metz and Bertrand de Poulangy had both encouraged her to put on male clothing ; but throughout her examinations, whenever a straight-forward reply might have recoiled injuriously on any of her old companions, she was either dumb or evasive.

Beaupère then inquired of her journey into France, and her coming to the king. She briefly recounted her journey, and said that she arrived at Chinon without impediment ; and that when brought into Charles's presence, she knew him amongst the courtiers by the counsel of her *voices.*

" At that time, when the *voice* showed you your king, was there any light in the place ? "

" Pass that over, I pray you ! "

" Did you see any angel above the head of your king ? "

" Spare me, and pass that over."

The belief in some miraculous *sign* given to Charles VII. by the Maid was very wide spread. Alain Chartier, the king's chief secretary, in writing to a foreign prince, soon after Jeanne's arrival at the court, informed him that she had told his royal master something which made him as glad as if the Holy Spirit had visited him. The emissaries of the bishop who collected the informations for her trial, gained just enough inkling of the mystery to provoke an intense curiosity amongst her persecutors to know more. It was made one of the main points of examination; and between Jeanne's loyal resolve to keep the king's secret, and their urgent desire to know it, her feet were entangled in a net, out of which she never had strength to extricate them, until she was brought face to face with death.

Beaupère having introduced the topic, would not let it go for all her pleading. He pressed her with question on question, insidiously varying their form, until he had extorted from her some words to the effect that before Charles set her to work, he had many beautiful apparitions and revelations. He asked her what these beautiful apparitions and revelations were.

"I shall not tell you. Up to the present hour, I have no right to answer you on that; but send to the king, and let him tell you himself what they were."

Beaupère still sedulously plying her on the same point, elicited that her own party fully believed her *counsel* was of God.

" My *voice* had promised me that the king would receive me very soon after I arrived near him," said she. " Those of my side knew well that the *voice* was sent me on the part of God—I am certain of it."

" Let us know what final recompense your *counsel* has promised you."

" I have never asked of my *counsel* any final recompense, but the salvation of my soul."

The examiner took up another theme — the assault on Paris. In reply to his questions, Jeanne said, " The *voice* bade me stay at Saint-Denis, and I wished to stay ; but against my will I was made to leave. But I should not have left had I not been wounded :—I was wounded in the moats at Paris ; in five days, however, I was healed. Yes, I made a skirmish before Paris."

" Was it not on a feast-day ? "

She confessed that it was.

" And do you think that was well done ? "

The Maid thought, no doubt, that every day was a good day to fight for her country ; but she only said, " Pass over that."

The bishop here stopped the interrogatory, and adjourned the court until Saturday.

The Third Session.

On Saturday twelve more ecclesiastics took their seats on the consistory, raising its number to sixty-three.

The bishop opened the morning's business with a stern injunction to the prisoner to make her oath without reservation. Thrice in vain he repeated his command. Then said Jeanne, " Give me leave to speak! By my faith, you may ask me many things touching my revelations about which I will not tell you the truth. If you constrain me to tell what I have sworn not to tell, you make me perjure myself, which you ought not to desire. Take heed what you do, since you say you are my judge ; for you take a great charge upon yourself, and much you burthen me."

The bishop offered her counsel to advise her whether she ought to swear as he bade her or not. She declined it. Then he told her that she made herself suspected by her refusal, and indeed exposed herself to be held convicted of the crimes of which she was accused. Threats could not daunt her.

" I am come on the part of God, and have nothing to do here!" exclaimed she, passionately. "You are not my judges. Leave me to the judgment of God, who sent me !"

" You are putting yourself in great peril," said the bishop ; and he admonished her again, and yet again, to swear.

At last, taking up some words of his own, she replied, " I am ready to tell you the truth on what I know concerns the trial," and in this form her oath was received. Raoul Sauvage, a civil lawyer on the consistory, declared that he never saw a woman of Jeanne's age give her examiners so much trouble as she did.

The debate with the bishop ended, Jean Beaupère began the interrogatory with his theory in his mind, by asking Jeanne at what hour she had last eaten and drunk.

"Since yesterday afternoon I have not eaten or drunk anything," replied she.

"How long is it since you heard the *voice* that comes to you?"

"I heard it yesterday, and I have heard it again to-day."

"At what hour did you hear it yesterday?"

"I heard it three times; once in the morning, once in the evening, and the third time when the *Ave Maria* was ringing. I hear it much oftener than I can tell you."

"What were you doing yesterday morning when the *voice* came to you?"

"I was sleeping, and it awoke me."

"Did it wake you by touching your arm?"

"No, it woke me without touching me."

"Was the *voice* in your chamber?"

"Not that I know of, but it was in the castle."

"Did you kneel then, and thank the *voice?*"

"I thanked it, sitting up in my bed, and clasping my hands."

" Why did it come ?"

" Because I had asked its help."

" And what did it bid you do ?"

" It bade me answer you boldly."

" What did it say to you at the moment it woke you ?"

" I begged its counsel on what I ought to answer, praying it to inquire of God. And the *voice* told me to answer you boldly, and God would help me."

" Had the *voice* spoken any words to you before you made it that prayer?"

"It had spoken some words, but I did not understand them all. Immediately I awoke, it said, *Answer boldly.*" As Jeanne quoted the advice of her *counsel*, she turned from Beaupère, and addressed the bishop : for the second time warning him that she knew what was in his heart against her. " You *say* that you are my judge :—*you are my adversary.* Be mindful what you do ; for verily I am sent on the part of God, and you are putting yourself in great danger."

" The king has commanded me to make your trial, and I shall make it," replied the bishop.

The Maid's denunciation of her judge as her adversary was not forgotten. There was a minute or two of confused silence in the court after he had spoken, and then Beaupère resumed the interrogatory.

" Does not that *voice* sometimes vary in its counsels ? "

"Never have I found the least contradiction in its words. Last night again it bade me answer boldly."

"Is it the *voice* that has forbidden you to reply to certain things that might be asked of you?"

"I have revelations concerning the king that I will not tell you."

"Has the *voice* forbidden you to tell those revelations?"

"I am not advised to answer you on that. . . . . Give me fifteen days' delay, and I will answer you then. . . . . Men have not forbidden me to speak of them. . . . . I do not know whether I ought to speak of them until it is revealed to me. . . . . I cannot answer you to-day." . . . .

Beaupère had the interrogatory now no longer to himself. The Maid's revelations about the king excited a restless anxiety amongst his brother-counsellors to get in a question. Sometimes two or three began to speak together, and a fourth and fifth would strike in before their predecessors were answered. The notaries had no chance. Jeanne had no chance either. She was faint with fasting. The impatient hurry fatigued and perplexed her; and at a moment when the confusion of tongues was loudest, she held her peace, and gave up trying to reply to any of them. They naturally came to a pause also, and she availed herself of the silence to say, "Pray, sirs, speak one after the other;" and then she appealed to the bishop not to let more than two at a time question her.

They had, however, by their united pressure, forced from her one very strong declaration with regard to her mysterious *counsel.* " Yes, I believe firmly, as firmly as I believe the Christian faith, and that God has redeemed us from the pains of hell, that the *voice* comes from God, and by His command."

The counsellors now moderated their tumult, and Beaupère was permitted to take up the word again. " Is the *voice* that appears to you, the voice of an angel, or a voice coming direct from God, or the voice of a saint ?"

" The *voice* comes on the part of God. I do not tell you clearly what I know about it, because I am more afraid to err in saying something that might displease the *voices* than I am of not answering you."

"Do you believe you would displease God by telling the truth ?"

" The *voices* have told me to tell certain things to the king, and not to you. Last night they told me many things for his good that I wish he knew, though I were to drink but water from now till Easter ; for if he knew them, he would be all the more happy to-day at his dinner !"

" Could you not persuade the *voice* to obey you, and carry that news to your king ? "

" I do not know whether the *voice* would consent or whether it might be the will of God.   Ah! if it pleased God, *He* could cause it to be revealed to my king, and I should be very glad of it!"

" Why does not the *voice* speak any more to your king, as it spoke when you were in his presence?"

" I do not know.   If it were not for the grace of God, I should not myself know how to act."

" During the two last days when you have heard the *voices*, did any light appear?"

" Light comes with the *voices*."

" When you see the *voices*, do you see anything else with them?"

" I cannot tell you all; I have not permission, and my oath does not comprehend that.   I demand that I may have given to me in writing the questions upon which I have yet to answer."

No notice was taken of Jeanne's requisition; Beaupère went on to ask if the *voice* of which she required counsel had a face and eyes.   A spark of Jeanne's old vivacity flashed out, and she replied, " You will not learn that from me now.   I have not forgotten what is said to little children—that sometimes people have been hanged for telling the truth!"

Beaupère referring to her former words, that if it were not for the grace of God, she should not know how to act, inquired here if she knew herself to be in the grace of God.

Jean Fabri, an Augustine monk, who sat on the consistory, interposed at this question, saying, " That is a great matter to answer—perhaps the accused is not bound to answer upon it."

" You would have done better to be silent," exclaimed the bishop, angrily.

Another scene of confusion ensued. Several of the counsellors, the Abbot of Feçamp amongst the most eager, insisted that the question was reasonable, and that the prisoner was under the necessity of replying. The anxiety of Fabri to defend her from it, warned Jeanne that it concealed a danger. Her perpetual prayer was to be taught how to answer these churchmen. The question was put to her again, " Speak, Jeanne, do you know yourself to be in the grace of God ? "

" If I am not, God bring me to it!" cried she. " If I am, God keep me in it ! I should be of all the world most miserable if I knew myself to be out of the love and favour of God !" The pathetic earnestness and piety of her words startled and confused her evil-wishers, and made the Augustine monk believe that surely she was inspired.

" Jeanne, thou hast answered well!" exclaimed another priest on the consistory—Hûlot de Châtillon, archdeacon of Evreux.

The silence that followed spoke the general assent of the hearers. There was so long a pause before the interrogatory was resumed that the notary.

Boisguillaume, detailing the scene many years afterwards, was under the impression that the court had
broken up, and dispersed for that day. The examination was, however, still continued, though on a different subject. The instruction for the trial tended
to prove that Jeanne's *voices* were not voices from
heaven, but the voices of demons; and Beaupère had
this in view when he proceeded to question her about
her childhood. He asked again when she first began
to hear them. She answered as before—when she
was about thirteen. He then inquired whether,
when she was little, she walked and played in the
fields with other children. This carried her back
to Domremy. Beaupère had no difficulty in making her talk of her village and her home. The
churchmen listened with all their ears while the
famous Maid recounted the simple story of her life
in Lorraine; betraying how, from her earliest years,
had fermented in her mind the great thoughts and
passions that urged her to the deliverance of France.

"Were the people of Domremy Burgundians, or
of the other party?" the examiner asked.

"I do not know that there was at Domremy
more than one Burgundian; and if it had pleased
God, I should have been glad to see his head cut
off," replied Jeanne, uncompromisingly.

"Did the *voice* bid you hate the Burgundians?"

"After I understood that the *voices* were for the
King of France, I did not love them."

" Had you a revelation from the *voice* in your childhood, that the English were to come into France?"

" The English were already in France when the *voices* began to visit me."

" Did you ever go out with the little children who fought for the side you held?"

" Not that I remember. But I have seen the boys of Domremy, who had fought with the boys of Marcey, come back sometimes wounded, and covered with blood."

" Had you at that time a great desire to injure the Burgundians?"

" I had a great desire and affection that my king should have his kingdom."

From this topic Beaupère passed to her daily occupations and amusements, and asked first, if it had been her task to drive the flocks and herds to pasture.

" After I reached years of discretion, I did not generally tend the cattle," said Jeanne ; " but I often helped to conduct them to the meadows, or to a castle called the *The Island*, for fear of the Burgundian foragers. Whether I kept the flocks in my childhood, I do not well remember."

" What is that marvellous tree near your village?"

" There is a tree called the *Beautiful May*—others call it the *Tree of the Fairies*, near which is a fountain.   People ill of any fever used to send for the water of the spring to heal them ; I have myself known them to do so, and when they were well enough to rise, they came to walk about the tree. It is a very great tree, a beech, and belongs to the knight Pierre de Bourlemont.   I have heard old women say—not any of my kindred—that once there were fairies there; my godmother, the wife of Maire Aubry, even said she had seen them.   I do not know whether it was true.   I never saw any there myself, or elsewhere that I know of."

The examiner inquired about the Fête of the Fountains, and what part Jeanne took in the sports.

"I hung my garlands on the branches of the tree as other girls did, and I danced and sang round it with them when I was young ; but after I knew I had to come into France, I do not remember ever to have danced.   I always sang more than I danced, and I took as little part in the sports as I could, when I grew up."

Beaupère asked her if there was not a fairy-haunted wood near Domremy.

"There is a wood called the Oak-wood, with glades in it where the cattle run, which can be seen from my father's door.   It is not half a league dis-tant.   I never heard that there were fairies there ; but my brother Jean has told me that they say in my country, I began my fate under the fairy-tree —the Beautiful May.   It is not true, and I am

grieved at it. When I came to the king also, several persons asked me if there was not in my country
a wood called *the Oak-wood;* because there were
prophecies which said, that from near that wood
ought to come a Maid who should do wonders."

Perhaps Jeanne broke down a little in the midst
these happy memories, and forgot in whose hands
she was; for when Beaupère asked suddenly:
"Jeanne, would you like to have a woman's dress
again?" she replied: "Give me one—I will put it
on, and go home to my mother!"

There was no response from the crowd of her
judges. She came to herself again, and added: "I
cannot put it on here. I am content with this,
since God is pleased that I should wear it."

The bishop at this point adjourned the court,
fixing the following Tuesday for the next session.

There had just arrived in Rouen a famous Norman lawyer, Jean Lohier, whose opinion the Bishop
of Beauvais was extremely anxious to obtain on
the Maid's trial. He sent for him to his house
that afternoon, and deputed Thomas de Courcelles
to show him the register of it as far as it had gone.
Lohier had already heard more of the cause than
he liked, and would fain have evaded the demand
for his opinion. The bishop, however, insisted on
his going into the business there and then; and
Lohier proceeded to study the register, and to

listen to Thomas de Courcelles' elucidations. He
then asked two or three days' leisure to consider
over it, but the bishop impatiently demanding his
views at once, the reluctant lawyer made a short
end by telling him that his beautiful trial was nothing worth. The judge irefully and anxiously
begged to know why.

" In the first place," replied Lohier, " it has not
the form of an ordinary trial. In the second, you
are carrying it on with closed doors, where the
counsel and assistants have not full and free liberty
to speak. In the third, you treat in it of things
concerning the honour of the King of France, of
whose party the Maid is, without calling him, or
any in his name. And in the last, neither bill nor
articles have been given to the accused, as the law
in trials for the faith requires ; nor any counsel to
direct her, who is but a simple girl, in answering
the masters and doctors in such great and delicate
matters as those she calls her *revelations*. For
each and all of these reasons, your trial seems to
me invalid."

The bishop burst into angry exclamation and
remonstrance, and concluded by telling Lohier he
should stay in Rouen to see the trial finished.
Lohier replied that he certainly should *not*—he had
business elsewhere, and would have no hand in
such a prosecution if he had ever so much leisure.
He was not a man to be daunted with threats, or

bribed to hold his peace, and reluctantly letting
him go, the bishop set off himself with De Courcelles to seek the rest of the Paris counsellors who
were lodged near the castle. Loiselleur and the
notary Manchon were there at the time.

Coming in amongst the doctors with haste and
undissembled rage, the prelate exclaimed : " Here
is Lohier, who would put us to a fine non-plus with
our trial ! He wants to slander it, and says it is
nothing worth. If we believe him, we must begin
all over again, and what we have done must go for
nothing." He then detailed the objections Lohier
had raised against their procedure, and added significantly : " It is easy to see on which foot *he*
halts. By St. John ! we will change nothing for
him ; we will carry on our trial as we have begun it."

Pierre Cauchon was a more noted lawyer than
even the Norman who had given him such an un-
palatable opinion on his work. His reputation,
and the reputation of his counsellors from Paris University, would outweigh many bad opinions of it.
Lohier had told De Courcelles that it was palpably
illegal to try a prisoner for the faith without such
previous informations of heresy as the promoter
did not possess. But De Courcelles looked up to
the bishop, and was content to follow his lead.
Nicole Midy was embarrassed with as few scruples
as the judge ; and Beaupère, Morrice, Texier, and

Feuillet, sagacious enough to know that in such a
case as the Maid's opinions were sure to differ,
appear to have been quite satisfied to advise him
according to his and their own political interests,
and to go on with the trial as they would have
gone on with any other, for which, in the way of business, they had been retained by a handsome fee.

The next morning Manchon, in the cathedral,
encountered Lohier.   What he had heard the
bishop say to the Paris doctors, and the opinion he
had formed for himself of his motives and *animus*
in the trial, made the notary desirous of hearing the
Norman lawyer's ideas on the same point.   He
asked him what he thought of the case altogether.

"You see the fashion in which they are going
on," replied Lohier.   "They will catch her in her
words.   She says of her *voices* and revelations *I am
certain*.   Now if she said, *It seems to me*, instead of
I am certain, it is my opinion that no man could
condemn her.   They appear to be moving against
her for hatred rather than anything else, and that is
why I will not meddle nor take any part in their trial."

On the morrow, notwithstanding a requisition
from the bishop to remain, Lohier quitted Rouen
on his way to Rome.   He died there a few years
later dean of the *Rota*, the papal court of appeal.

The Fourth Session.

As Massieu was conducting Jeanne to the court

on the Tuesday morning, he permitted her, as he had done before, to rest a few minutes in front of the chapel to pray. Jean d'Estivet happened to pass and see her, and coming up to the kind-hearted priest, he said brutally, " How dare you let that excommunicated wretch approach the church ? If you do it again, I will give you a prison for a month, where you shall see neither sun nor moon." He then went away to the hall, whither the prisoner followed. Massieu did not heed his threats.

Eighteen of the assessors who had sat on the consistory on Saturday had now absented them-selves, and some of them never rejoined it. The bishop this morning avoided an argument with Jeanne about the oath by permitting her to swear in her own way ; and Beaupère, before beginning his formal interrogatory, inquired in what state of health she had been since Saturday? She did not take it in good part.

" You see in what health I am," replied she. " I am as well as it is possible for me to be."

" Have you fasted each day of this Lent ? "

" Does that concern your trial ? " She was told that it did, and then she said, " Yes, I have fasted always this Lent."

Being asked if she had heard her *voice* since Saturday, she answered that she had heard it many times ; and also that she had need of it.

" Did you hear it on Saturday in this hall where you are interrogated ? "

" Yes, I heard it here, but I understood nothing that I can recite to you until I returned to my room. . . . . Then it bade me answer you boldly, and I prayed for counsel on the things you ask me. I will readily tell you what God permits me to tell; but as to the revelations touching the King of France, of them I will tell nothing."

" Is it the voice of an angel, of a saint, or the voice of God without a medium that comes to you ?"

" The *voice* is that of St. Katherine and St. Margaret. Their faces are crowned with beautiful crowns, very rich, and very precious. Of that I have leave of my Lord to speak. If you doubt me, send to Poitiers, where also I wâs examined : it is written in a register there."

This response gave Beaupère a new clue. He asked Jeanne how she discerned one saint from the other, if they were both dressed alike, how long she had known them, if they were of her own age, if they spoke at the same time or separately, and which of them came to her first. By dint of perseverance, he wrung from her the name of St. Michael as the earliest of her angelic visitants, and that he came to her not alone, but attended by a great company of the heavenly host.

" Did you see St. Michael and the angels corporally and really ? "

" I saw them with my bodily eyes as well as I see you. When they left me I wept, and fain would I that they had borne me away with them!"

" What did St. Michael say to you the first time he appeared?"

" I have not permission at present to tell you. . . . . Of course, I told my king what had been revealed to me, because it regarded him. I wish you had a copy of that book at Poitiers."

" Did God command you to dress as a man?"

" My man's dress is a very trifling matter—the most trifling. I did not put it on by the advice of any man in the world. Whatever I have done of good, I have done by command of God and the saints. . . . . . I would rather have been torn by wild horses than have come into France without the permission of God. . . . . If He ordered me to put on another habit, I should put it on. . . . . In all that I have done by His command, I believe I have done well, and, therefore, I look for His good keeping and good help."

The examiner here inquired again if, with the *voice*, light appeared. Jeanne replied that there was a great light, but that it did not come for him. Jacques Tiphaine, one of the physicians from Paris, marvelled at her audacity of speech that morning ; and Jacques Texier came to the aid of his brother-counsellor, and questioned her too.

" Was there any angel above the head of your
king when you saw him for the first time ? "

" By the blessed Mary, if there was I do not
know; I saw none."

" Was there any light there ? "

" There were more than three hundred chevaliers,
and fifty flambeaux, besides the spiritual light."

" How did your king come to put faith in your
words ? "

" He had good signs to believe them. I was interrogated by the clergy during three weeks at
Chinon and Poitiers ; and the opinion of the ecclesiastics of my party was, that they saw nothing but
good in my vocation."

" Were you ever at Saint-Katherine-de-Fier-
bois ? "

" Yes; and I heard three masses there in one day."

She was then questioned about the discovery of
her famous sword, and she said : " When I was at
Tours, I wrote to the ecclesiastics of Fierbois, to
beg them to let me have a sword which was in the
church of St. Katherine, behind the altar. It was
in the earth, and rusty ; there were five crosses on
it, and I knew it was there by my *voices*. I think
it was not very deep in the earth ; and immediately
it was found, the ecclesiastics had it rubbed, and
the rust fell off easily. It was an armourer of
Tours, whom I had never seen, who went to seek
it. The ecclesiastics of Fierbois gave me a red

velvet scabbard for it, and those of Tours gave me another of cloth of gold ; and a third I had made myself, of very strong leather."

"Did you not sometimes lay that sword on the altar, and pray that it might be fortunate ? "

" I never laid it on the altar that I know of ; but, of course, I prayed that all my arms might have good luck."

"Did you wear that sword at the time of your capture ? "

" No. . . . . Where I left it, I shall not tell you, for it does not concern your trial. I loved that sword very much, because it had been found in the church of St. Katherine, whom I love. . . . . The sword I wore at Compiègne had been taken from a Burgundian ; a good sword of war it was, and good to give good *blows* and *clouts*."

Some of those solemn churchmen were affronted at the fervour with which Jeanne described her weapons of war, and fancied she was making a mock at them with her *blows* and her *clouts*. In the summing up of her iniquities she heard of them again. She was guilty of several little sallies of spirit and temper during this interrogatory.

Her Standard, its material, its colour, painting, and inscription of JHESUS MARIA were the next theme of the inquisitors, and Jeanne was asked which she liked best to carry—her Standard or her sword.

" I liked to carry my Standard forty times better than my sword. And I always carried my Standard myself when I attacked the enemy, to avoid killing any one ; and, indeed, I never did kill any one."

Jacques Texier, the mild Franciscan, asked her with an air of solicitude if she had ever really found herself where the English were being slain. Jeanne answered him in a tone of half-laughing contempt : " That have I ! How meekly you talk ! Why did they not quit France, and begone into their own country ? "

An English lord, who happened to be standing near where sat on the consistory Jacques Tiphaine and Guillaume Desjardins, said aloud : " Truly she is a good woman—if only she were English ! "

Beaupère continued his investigations into the Maid's martial exploits. It could not be altogether disagreeable to him or any of her persecutors— being French—to hear her recount how she had beaten the English ; and Jeanne answered his questions with evident zest.

" How many men did your king entrust you with when he set you to work ? "

" From ten to twelve thousand. At the raising of the siege of Orleans I began with the bastile of Saint-Loup, and finished with that of the bridge. I knew by revelation that I should raise the siege, and so I told the king before I went."

" Did you not say to your men, when you led them to the attack, that *you* would receive the arrows, and bolts, and the stones from the bombards and cannons?"

"Truly, no! On the contrary, a hundred or more were wounded there; but I bade my soldiers often to have no fear, and they would raise the siege. I, myself, in the assault on the Tournelles, was wounded in the neck by an arrow; but St. Katherine comforted me, and in fifteen days I was well. I did not leave off riding, or going about my business at all. I was the first to raise a ladder against the rampart, and it was in raising it that I was wounded."

"Why did you not receive to treaty the Earl of Suffolk, the commander at Jargeau?"

"He asked a fortnight's truce, which the lords of my party would not grant; but they said the English might march out with their arms and horses if they went at once. But as for me, I said they should save their lives only, and begone in their smocks, or I would take them by assault."

" Did you deliberate with your *counsel* whether to grant them that truce or not?"

"I do not remember."

At this point of the interrogatory, the bishop adjourned the court to the following Thursday.

The Fifth Session.

On the Thursday morning, as Massieu and Jeanne drew near the chapel on their way to the tribunal, they saw Jean d'Estivet planted in front of the door to prevent her resting there. Jeanne looked at the wicked priest, and said, significantly, as she passed : " Is not the body of Jesus Christ there ? "*

At the opening of this session there was another long argument between the judge and the prisoner about the oath, Jeanne firmly refusing to swear unconditionally. She prevailed again, and her oath was accepted with the former limit—that she would speak truth on all points that she knew belonged to her trial. "And on them," said she, " I will reply to you as fully as if I were before the Pope of Rome."

"What do you say of our lord the Pope ? Which do you believe is the true Pope ? " asked Beaupère. Jeanne answered him with an inquiry whether there were two. He did not reply, but asked her if the Count of Armagnac had not written to her to know which of the three sovereign pontiffs, disputing the year before last, he ought to obey.

" The count did write to me on that subject, and I sent him word, amongst other things, that when I should be in Paris, or elsewhere at rest, I would

---

* The Eucharist exposed on the altar.

answer him. I was about to mount my horse when I gave that reply."

The bishop caused a copy of her letter to be read, and asked if it was hers. She said she thought it was hers in part, but she could not remember it all, and did not believe it was all hers. After some cross-examination about her views of the Pope, which elicited only that she held to him who lived at Rome, she was asked if she was not in the practice of putting a cross and the words JHESUS MARIA at the head of her letters.

"I put them in some, and in others not. Sometimes I put *one* cross, which signified that those of my party to whom I wrote were not to do what I sent orders for,"—letters, *these*, designed apparently to fall into the hands of the enemy, and to mislead them. Jeanne had learnt the manœuvres of war before her career ended, averse to everything of the sort as she was at the beginning of it.

Her letter of summons to Henry VI., the Duke of Bedford, and the generals before Orleans, was then read, and she was asked if she recognised it. She said she did, all but three phrases.

"Instead of *surrender to the Maid*, it should be, *surrender to the king;* and *chief of war* and *hand to hand* were not in the letter that I sent."

These expressions do, however, occur in the best-authenticated copies of that famous document, and though they might sound too arrogant to be true

when the Maid stood there, a prisoner in the hands
of those she had menaced, they no more than
echoed the voice of her inspiration when it was
triumphant. But even her own memory of her
glorious deeds was becoming tarnished with prison-
dust; and when her brave words were recited to
her, she did not know them again, though her pro-
phetic assurance that France should be delivered
from the English was as strong in her heart still,
as when she set forth in the name of God to deliver it. Amidst the many things that failed her,
that great hope for her country never wavered an
instant; and when her interrogators made some
derisive comments on her menaces, and asked how
now were they to be fulfilled, she answered them
with a solemn foresight which many there lived to
acknowledge and see verified.

"Before seven years are at an end, the English
shall abandon a greater gage than they abandoned
before Orleans, and they shall lose all in France.
. . . . Greater ruin shall come upon them than
ever they have had yet, and it shall be by a victory that God will give the French."

"How do you know this?"

"I know it by the revelation that has been made
to me. Before seven years are over, it shall come
to pass; and very wroth am I that it is so long delayed."

"On what day will it happen?"

"I know neither the day nor the hour."

"In what year?"

"That I shall not tell you. I wish it were to be before Mid-summer!"

"Did you not say to John Grey, your guard, that it would happen before Martinmas?"

"I said to him that many things would be seen before Martinmas, and that perhaps it would be the English who should be cast down to the ground."

"By whom do you know this event that is to be in the future?"

"By St. Katherine and St. Margaret."

Jeanne's mention of her saints diverted the interrogatory into another long cross-examination on their aspect. In answer to a multiplicity of questions, some foolish, some captious, some impertinent, she said, "I see them always in the same form. . . . . I see a face. . . . . I do not know if there is anything in the shape of arms or other members figured. . . . They are crowned; of their other vestments I cannot speak. . . . . I know them by the sound of their voices. . . . . They are sweet and humble. . . . . They speak very well, and in beautiful language, and I understand them perfectly."

"Does St. Margaret speak English?"

"How should she speak English when she is not of the English party?"

" These heads crowned that you see, have they rings in their ears ? "

" I do not know."

" Yourself, have not you some rings ? "

Jeanne turned to the bishop, and said, " You have one that is mine. The Burgundians have another that belongs to me."

" Who gave you that ring the Burgundians have ? "

"My father and mother at Domremy. The words *Jhesus Maria* are written on it. My brother gave me the other ring that *you* have ; I charge you to give it to the Church."

" Did St. Katherine and St. Margaret ever converse with you under the fairy-tree?" asked Beaupère.

" I do not know."

" Did they ever speak to you by the fountain near that tree ? "

" Yes, I have heard them in that place, but I do not know what they said to me then."

" What have those saints promised you, there or elsewhere ? "

" That does not concern your trial. . . . Amongst other things, they tell me my king shall recover his kingdom whether his adversaries will or no ; and me they have promised to guide to paradise, as I have prayed of them. They promise me nothing but by the permission of God."

" Has your *counsel* promised that you shall be

delivered out of prison?—out of the prison where you are now?"

"Ask me three months hence, and I will answer you." She was bidden to answer at once, and on her protesting that the question did not import to the trial, she was assured by many of the counsellors that it did. She grew impatient. A haunting presentiment of death moved shadow-like amongst her hopes; but though she dared not deny it, she strove hard not to betray it. Her reply was evasive, "I have always told you that you cannot know all—needs must that I shall be once delivered! Those who would put me out of this world, may go before me."

"Have your *voices* forbidden you to speak the truth?"

"Do you wish me to tell what is sent only to the king of France? I know many things that do not concern this trial. . . . . I know that the king shall recover all the kingdom of France; I know that as well as I know that you are there. I should be dead, but for the revelation that comforts me every day!"

The examiner took up another theme, and asked the hapless prisoner, "What she had done with her *mandragora?*"

"I have none, and never have had any," was her indignant reply.

The instruction of the trial went to prove that

she was the depositary of a mandragora, and hence her past good fortune. The collectors of the informations had heard of the fabled plant at Domremy; and there was another rumour in circulation of Brother Richard having compelled a number of persons to burn some that they kept hidden in secret places:—perhaps Jeanne amongst them, to burn hers, might be implied.

In answer to some further questions on this point, she said, " I have heard that there was one near my village, ... in the earth near the tree that has been spoken of; but I do not know the spot. I have also heard that above it grew a hazel-bush. I was told that it was a very bad and perilous thing to keep."

" And what were you told that mandragora served for ? "

" I have heard say that it made money come, but I never believed it."

" Did your *voices* speak to you about it ? "

" No, my *voices* never told me anything about it."

This point was a signal failure. The interrogatory had not yet succeeded in obtaining any evidence that the prisoner's *counsel* gave advice such as might be expected from demons. Beaupère reverted to her mysterious apparitions, and bade her describe of what aspect St Michael was when he came to her.

"I did not see that he had a crown ; and of his vestments I know nothing," said she.

"Then was he naked, Jeanne ?"

"Do you imagine that God has not withal to clothe him ?"

Beaupère, disconcerted for a moment, went on to ask if the angel had hair.

"Why should he have had it cut off?" retorted Jeanne, with impatient contempt. "I do not know whether he had hair or not. I never saw him often, and I have not seen him at all since I came away from the castle of Crotoy. . . . . I feel a great joy when I do see him ; and it appears to me that I am not then in mortal sin. St. Katherine and St. Margaret make me confess from time to time, and turn by turn."

"Do you believe that you are in mortal sin when you confess?"

Hûlot de Châtillon here raised his voice from the tribunal and said, *that* question ought not to be put to the accused. The bishop bade him not interrupt the interrogatory. "I must acquit my conscience," returned the archdeacon. He had made objections before to some of the questions, as Jean Fabri had done, and the counsellors from Paris had complained of his interference. There was some angry debate now, which the bishop stopt by dismissing Châtillon from the consistory, with an injunction not to come any more until he

was sent for. He came, however, the next day as
if nothing had happened; but the incident gave
rise to many invidious remarks on the temper of
the judge, who proposed to discard from his tribunal one of the very few persons on it, who were
disposed, or who were bold enough, to show any
watchfulness over the prisoner.

When silence was restored, Jeanne was required
to say whether she believed herself to be in mortal
sin. She, penetrated with religious faith as she
was, was yet so ignorant of its terms and phrases,
that she did not detect the traps set for her in such
questions; but some of the assessors, talking her
over amongst themselves, vowed that the wisest
doctor of them all could hardly have answered with
more prudence. The insidious demand now made
on her conscience, she met as well as she had met
the demand to say whether she was in a state of
grace.

"I do not know if I am in mortal sin, and I do
not believe I have done its works. Please God
that I never may have been in it! Please God
that I never may do, or may have done, such
deeds as shall burthen my soul!"

After this answer, which ill-accorded with the
theory of the prosecution, that the Maid was a
monster of pride and a familiar of demons, Beaupère abruptly asked her, perhaps hoping to take
her by surprise: "What sign did you give to your

king, that you came on the part of God?" But Jeanne was not easily taken by surprise.

"I have always told you that you shall extort nothing from me about that. Go, and ask himself!" replied she.

"Have you not sworn to answer upon what concerns your trial?"

"I have said that I will tell you nothing that concerns the king. Of what belongs to him, or touches him, I will not speak!" She was assured that the sign given to Charles was a matter of her own trial. She persisted in her refusal to tell it. "I have promised to keep it secret, and I will. I could not tell it without perjury."

"To whom have you made that promise?"

"To St. Katherine and St. Margaret; and the king knows it. I made that promise to the two saints by my own desire, because a great many persons inquired of me about it, before I had pledged them my word never to speak of it."

"When you showed the sign to the king, were there any other persons in his company?"

"I think there was no one but myself, though there were numbers of people near."

"Did you see a crown on your king's head when you showed him the sign?"

"I cannot tell you without perjury."

"What crown had your king when he was at Rheims?"

" The king, I think, took with gratitude the crown that he found at Rheims; a very rich crown that was being brought to him, arrived after his departure.   He acted thus to hasten his business at the request of the people of Rheims, to whom a longer sojourn of the army would have been very onerous. But if he had waited, he would have had a crown a thousand times more rich."

" Did you see that crown, so much more rich than the other?"

" If I did not see it, I have, at least, heard say that it is, by God's grace, very rich and opulent."

The bishop at this point stopt the interrogatory, and adjourned the court until Saturday.

As Jean Massieu was leaving the castle, after he had re-conducted Jeanne to her prison, he fell in with a priest named Eustache Turquetil, very eager in his curiosity, as it appeared, to learn how matters were likely to go with her.   " What do you think of her answers?   Will she be burned?   How will it be?" asked he.

The usher was taken off his guard.   " Thus far I have seen only good and honour in her," replied he.   " But I do not know what she may come to in the end.   God knows."

Turquetil, who was English in his prejudices, repeated Massieu's incautious opinion to some of the Earl of Warwick's people, and it was immediately carried to the ears of the bishop.   In the afternoon the prelate sent for Massieu, and gave him a sharp rebuke, warning him that he would get into trouble if he did not take heed what he said. Jean d'Estivet had also preferred a complaint of the usher's kindness to the prisoner in letting her pray at the chapel-door, and he was charged by the judge to permit her the indulgence no more.

The Sixth Session.

On Saturday morning there appeared on the consistory another famous doctor and deputy for the Council of Bâle, Guillaume Erard, a canon of Beauvais, and treasurer and canon of the cathedral of Langres. His presence at the Maid's trial was perhaps more pernicious to her than that of any other assessor whom the Bishop of Beauvais summoned. The total number had now declined to forty. The sessions of the court were long and tedious, and likely to be longer and more tedious still before the cause was concluded.

The judge endeavoured to get an unconditional oath from Jeanne, but she would only swear as she had sworn before, and he was obliged to yield the point again. The interrogatory opened straight-way upon the subject of St. Michael and her other apparitions.

"I have told you all I know of them, and I can tell you no more," replied Jeanne. "I have seen St. Michael and the two saints so well, that I know they are saints of paradise. I have seen them with my bodily eyes, and I believe they are saints as firmly as I believe that God exists."

"Do you know by revelation that you shall escape?"

"That does not concern your trial. Do you wish me to speak against myself? If all imported to you, I would tell you all. . . . . By my faith, I know neither the day nor the hour when I shall escape. I leave it to my Lord!"

"But have not your *voices* told you something about it in a general way?"

"Yes, truly. They have told me that I shall be delivered, (but I know neither the day nor the. hour,) and that I may boldly wear a cheerful countenance!"

Beaupère now took up the topic of her male habit, questioning her very closely to extort some direct confession that it had been put on at the bidding of her *voices*. He failed completely; for, after he had tried every masked approach to surprise what he wanted, he tried a point-blank attack, demanding whether, when God revealed to her that she must change her dress, it was by the *voice* St. Michael, St. Katherine, or St. Margaret, and Jeanne said, with decision, that she would not answer another question on the subject. He then shifted his line of interrogatory to her imaginary enchantments; and, after several questions about her

Standard, he asked if she had not told the soldiers that pennons like those of her company were fortunate.

The Maid had no reason to hide her witchcraft, such as it was. She told him how she and her soldiers were fortunate: "I said to my men, *Go in amongst the English boldly!* and I went myself."

The examiner made some further inquiries about the pennons of her companions-in-arms—whether she had them sprinkled with holy water, carried in procession round a church, and inscribed with her monogram of JHESUS MARIA. Jeanne said if they were so sprinkled, carried, and inscribed, it was not by her orders.

"When you were before Jargeau, did you not wear something round at the back of your casque?"

"No, by my faith, there was nothing on it!" That Jeanne escaped without hurt from the great stone flung down on her, which was broken on her head into a multitude of pieces, wore quite the appearance of sorcery to the English soldiers; and in that light her ecclesiastical judges also regarded it.

She was then asked if she knew Brother Richard. She described the manner of his receiving her at Troyes. No mischief could be made out of that, and Beaupère went on to inquire if she had not caused images or pictures to be made in her like-ness.

" I never caused any image or picture to be made in my likeness, and never saw but one—at Arras, painted by a Scot. It represented me in arms, kneeling on one knee, and presenting a letter to the king."

"What was that picture in your host's house at Orleans, where three women were painted, and in-scribed underneath, *Justice, Peace, Union ?* "

" I do not know anything about it."

" Do you not know that some of your party have had service, mass, and prayers for you ? "

" If they have had service, it was not by my command ; if they have prayed for me, I think they have not done amiss."

This part of the interrogatory was to prove that Jeanne had usurped divine honours. She was next asked if her own party really believed that she was sent on the part of God, and if she thought that a good belief ?

" I do not know *certainly* whether they believe it —that is, in their own hearts. If they do, they are not deceived ; if they do not, I am *still* sent on the part of God."

" Did you not understand very well the thought of those who kissed your feet, and hands, and clothes ? "

" If they kissed my hands and clothes, I could

not help it. The poor people came about me gladly, because I never did them any displeasure, but succoured them as I was able."

"Did not Brother Richard preach a sermon on your coming to Troyes?"

"I know nothing of any sermon there. I did not stop at Troyes, to rest or sleep at all."

"Have you not held children at the font in baptism?"

"Yes. At Troyes I held one; at Rheims I do not recollect any, nor at Chateau-Thierry; but at Saint-Dénis I stood for two. The boys I named *Charles*, in honour of my king, and the girls *Jeanne;* and sometimes I named them differently, as their mothers wished."

"Did not the good wives of Saint-Dénis touch their rings with the ring you wore?"

"Many, many women have touched my hands and my rings, but I do not know what was their intention.'

"What did you do with the gloves at Rheims, where your king was crowned?"

"There was a distribution of gloves to the knights and nobles there. And one of them lost his gloves . . . ."

"Did you not say you would cause them to be found again?"

"No, I never said so."

"When you were marching through the country, did you often receive the sacrament of the altar?"

" Yes, always on coming to a town."

" Did you receive it in your man's dress ? "

" Yes, but I do not remember ever to have received it in arms."

" Why did you take the Bishop of Senlis' mare ? "

" She was bought for two hundred crowns.
Whether he ever had them or not, I cannot say,
but he had a cheque to pay them. I wrote to
him afterwards that he might have her back if he
chose ; for I did not like her. She was good-for-
nothing to bear fatigue."

" What age was the child at Lagny that you went
to visit ? "

" Three days old. It was carried into the church
of Notre-Dame, and I was asked to go and pray
with other girls to God and Our Lady that they
would give it life. I went and prayed with the
rest. And at last life appeared, and it yawned
three times ; and then it was baptized, and immediately died, and was buried in holy ground. It
was said that for three days it had shown no life,
and it was as black as my dress ; but when it
yawned, the colour began to return into its face."

" Was it not said through the town that the child
was raised at *your* prayer ? "

" I never made any inquiry about it."

" Do not you know Katherine of Rochelle ? "

" Yes, I saw her at Jargeau and at Montfaucon,
in Berry."

"Did she not show you a lady dressed in white, who, she said, appeared to her sometimes?"

"No." Jeanne then gave a full account of her acquaintance with this adventuress, who, since the Maid's capture, had fallen herself into the hands of the ecclesiastical authorities at Paris. They had, however, marked their sense of her insignificance by letting her go again, after she had told a few substantial lies about the famous prisoner whom she had aspired to rival. An elder woman, taken with Katherine, who also had visions, had been burnt, while Jeanne was at Beaurevoir; one of her crimes being that she maintained Jeanne was good, and verily inspired of God to restore France to its rightful king.

"Did you not at La Charité cause water to be thrown on the ramparts after the manner of an aspersion?"

"No! I caused an assault to be made." Jeanne was charged, by and by, with showing irreverence to her reverend judges. Possibly a smile broke over her face at their notion of her attacking a strong town with an asperge and a pot of holy water.

"Were you long in the tower at Beaurevoir?"

"I was there four months, or nearly. When I knew the English were come, I was very much afflicted. My *voices* forbade me to fly many times; but at last, for fear of the English, I commended myself to God and Our Lady, and sprang from the tower. I was hurt, but the *voice* St. Katherine told me to be of good comfort, for I should recover, and the people of Compiègne should have succour. I prayed always with my *counsel* for those in Compiègne."

"When you were taken up, did you not blaspheme the name of God, and say you would rather die than be in the hands of the English?"

"I never blasphemed the name of God, nor the name of any saint. I am not accustomed to blaspheme, but I *would* rather give up my soul to God than be in the hands of the English!"

With this reply the public examinations of the Maid closed. She was re-conducted to her prison, and the Bishop of Beauvais, addressing the consistory, said, that not any longer to fatigue unnecessarily so great a number of assessors, he would call a few doctors and masters, skilled in divine and human law, to select amongst the confessions and assertions of the accused, those on which it might seem necessary to interrogate her further; and to them he would give a commission for her private examination. The whole would be put in writing, so that the other assessors might consult and deliberate over it, and give their opinions at convenient times. Meanwhile, they were invited to reflect at home over what they had already heard of the trial; and finally they were forbidden, each and all, to quit the city of Rouen, without the permission of the judge, until after it was concluded.

IV.

THE EXAMINATIONS IN PRISON.

HE following day, Sunday, the Paris counsellors and several more doctors and
masters met at the bishop's house to
review the assertions and confessions of the Maid
recorded in the registers of the notaries. These registers had been carefully compared at the close of
each examination, and the honesty of Manchon and
Boisguillaume prevented any serious falsification.
More than once in the course of the interrogatory,
the judge and his special counsellors had directed
them to omit certain of the prisoner's answers as
not being pertinent to the trial, and to write others
in a sense different from what they understood.
Manchon protested that he would write as he heard,
or not at all. At the daily revision of the registers,
the notes taken by the English secretaries were

produced, and Manchon complained that the pleas
and qualifications of the accused were omitted
from them. Frequent disputes arose as to who
was right and who was wrong in these cases, and
Manchon always refusing to yield the point, marked
them, that Jeanne might be re-questioned for a
certainty. His register was therefore up to this
period correct, or nearly so. Some strong remarks
of the accused, addressed to the judge, and the
objections raised by any bold assessor, had not
been recorded, but what was recorded was substan-
tially true.

The deliberation of the doctors over what had
been done in the trial continued six days, and was
not at all harmonious, though the bishop had the
power of summoning to it only whom he would.
The six counsellors from the University, and his
familiar and spy, Nicolas Loiselleur, were always
present. The majority of the other assessors served
on the trial as willingly as they ; some moved by
prejudice, some by self-interest ; but probably
more, imposed on by the specious dignity of the
tribunal, supposed themselves to be engaged in a
painful but necessary duty. Amongst the crowd
cited, however, there could hardly fail to be some
men sagacious, honourable, and high - spirited
enough to see through the bishop's designs, and
to mark their abhorrence of them. Amongst these,
the most conspicuous was Nicolas de Houppe-

ville, another Norman lawyer of distinction, who
met the judge with as bold rebuke and defiance as
Jean Lohier.   He told him frankly that, in his
opinion, neither he nor any of those who had
assumed the responsibility of trying the Maid,
were her competent judges, being of the party
opposed to her.   The Church was not neutral
ground, while the clergy were divided by such
animosities as prevailed in France.   He further
reminded Pierre Cauchon that the doctors and
divines of Poitiers had declared they found nothing
in her but what should be in a good Christian
and good Catholic, and that his own metropolitan,
the Archbishop of Rheims, had presided over the
commission that pronounced this opinion.

The judge might have replied with great show
of reason—Why does not the Archbishop of
Rheims, why do not the doctors and divines of
Poitiers, come forward and maintain that opinion,
if they still hold it?   We gave them long enough
warning.   The Court of Rome, the Council of
Bâle are open to their appeal.   In abandoning
her to us, do they not imply that we shall do her
justice?

What answer the bishop made to Nicolas de
Houppeville in words does not appear, but the
courageous lawyer found himself a day or two
after lodged in the king's prison.   When he inquired why he had been arrested, he was told that

it was at the request of the Bishop of Beauvais, and that he was very likely to be sent across to England out of the way. He possessed, however, an influential friend in the Abbot of Feçamp, and he recovered his liberty ; but this example of how the Maid's judge would deal with men bold enough to put impediments in the way of his beautiful trial, probably had its influence in keeping other doubtful or uneasy assistants in submissive good order.

On one point, however, the majority of the assessors, not being in the bishop's secrets, opposed his decision with much murmuring. They thought it very wrong to leave the accused in a secular prison while undergoing her trial before an ecclesiastical court, and suggested that she ought to be removed to the church-prison. The judge, however, evaded their advice, alleging that it would be an affront to the English to take her out of their custody. And in the castle she was left, guarded by her capital enemies : securely, fatally caged as ever poor prisoner was.

The council at the bishop's house brought their labours to a conclusion on Friday, the 9th of March. The points they drew out from the registers for the further examination of the Maid, included nearly all on which she had been already questioned, with the addition of several more taken from the informations for the trial.

The next morning, the judge went at eight o'clock to her prison, accompanied by two assessors only, Nicole Midy and Gerard Feuillet. The promoter, Jean d'Estivet, was present, and Jean Delafontaine, the bishop's clerk in ordinary, was there to conduct the interrogatory. Manchon attended as notary, and Massieu, the usher, and Jean Fécard, an advocate of the king's court, served as witnesses of the proceedings.

Jeanne was not relieved of her fetters while under examination in her prison, and though she had cause to complain of the excessive fatigue to which she was subjected, her great spirit showed no symptoms of breaking yet. The morning examinations were prolonged for three hours, and there was often a second held in the afternoon, nearly as tedious. And this continued for six days, to the close of the following week.

The bishop began business with his usual admonition to the prisoner to swear unconditionally, but she still refused, and he accepted her former limited oath. He had her now, however, more completely in his power than in the hall, where some conscientiously obstructive priest might at any moment interpose to help her; and if she continued obstinate, he had means of coercion near such as few could withstand. She was under a much greater disadvantage during these private examinations than she had been before the consistory; for he not only found opportunities of misleading her here, which would hardly have served him in the presence of the multitude of assessors, but also of hoodwinking and misleading the assessors themselves whose duty it would ultimately be to pronounce on her fate.

Jean Delafontaine opened the interrogatory by asking Jeanne from what place she set out when she went last to Compiègne.

" From Crépy, in Valois," said she.

" When you were come to Compiègne, was it many days before you made a sally?"

" I came in the morning before dawn, and entered the town unknown to the enemy; and the same day, towards evening, I made the sally in which I was taken."

" Were the bells rung at the sally?"

" If they were, it was not by my orders, or with my knowledge. I never thought of them, and do not remember to have bidden any one ring them."

" Was it at the command of your *voices* you sallied?"

" No. In Easter-week, last past, I was on the ramparts at Mélun, when it was told me by my *voices*, St. Katherine and St. Margaret, that I should be taken before the feast of St. John, but that I must not be afraid; for God would succour me."

" Did your *voices* afterwards, elsewhere besides at Mélun, tell you you would be taken?"

" Yes, many times—every day as it were. And I entreated them, when I should be taken, that I might soon die, without long sorrow in prison. I often asked to know the hour, but they did not tell me."

" If your *voices* had commanded you to make the sally, and had signified that you would be taken, should you have gone?"

" I should not have gone willingly, but I should have gone in the end, whatever was to befall me."

" In making the sally, did you pass beyond the bridge?"

" I crossed the bridge and the rampart, and rode with a company of my people against the lord of Luxembourg's men, and drove them back to their tents twice, and the third time half way. The English then took us in the rear, and cut off our retreat to the bridge; and I was drawing my men towards the fields Picardy-way, when I was taken."

" When you sallied, did you carry your Standard on which the world was painted?"

" Yes, I never had but one."

" Did you not bear a coat of arms?"

" No, I had none. But my king gave arms to my brothers—a shield of azure, two lilies of gold, and a sword in the midst. They were given to gratify them, without any request of mine."

" Who gave you the horse you rode when you were taken?"

" My king. I had five chargers bought with the king's money, besides nags, of which I had seven."

" Had you any other gifts from the king besides those horses?"

" I never asked of my king anything but good arms, good horses, and money to pay the people of my household."

" Had you not some treasure?"

" The ten or twelve thousand crowns I had were not much to carry on war—they were very little. I think my brothers have my horses and other property, but whatever money I have is the king's."

Thus far Jeanne had answered with perfect freedom, but the perilous theme of the *sign* she had given to Charles, was now introduced with a systematic design of forcing her to divulge it. That moral torture which a truthful soul writhes under, when urged to speak upon a matter of which it *dares* not speak plainly, and of which it *cannot* any longer refuse to speak at all, began to betray itself in her by evasions, broken allegories, contradictions, prevarications. Jeanne did not always speak the truth before her judges, but her metaphorical legends to hide it, tripped anything but glibly from her tongue.

" What is the sign that came to your king to make him believe you were sent on the part of God?" Delafontaine asked.

" It is beautiful and honourable, and much to be believed; and it is good, and the richest that can be," was her enigmatical answer.

To what the perfidious counsels Jeanne received from Nicolas Loiselleur tended, does not distinctly appear; but one piece of his advice might well be to endeavour to deceive her judges with a parable about the sign which they could readily convert into a net for herself. She had knotted the first meshes of it now, and had but to be insidiously wiled on to weave it out. She detected soon the snare she had spread for her own feet, and struggled again and again to free herself; but every effort only wound the clue more quickly, until she was completely laid fast in its labyrinthine tangles, and bound at the mercy of her adversaries.

" Why will you not tell that sign?" continued the interrogator. " You required Katherine of Rochelle to show you hers."

" If the sign of Katherine of Rochelle had been shown before the Archbishop of Rheims, and the other bishops whose names I do not know, and before Charles de Bourbon, and the Duke of Alençon, and the Sire de la Trémouille, and many knights besides, who heard and saw the king's sign as plainly as I see you speaking to me to-day, I should not have desired to see it."

" Does the sign still continue?" asked the bishop, assuming the examiner's office himself.

"It is good to know it does! It will last a thousand years and more; and it is in the king's treasury."

" Is it gold, silver, precious stones, or a crown?"

" I shall tell you no more about it—no man could know how to imagine anything so rich! But the sign *you* need is, that God should deliver me out of your hands, and it is the surest sign He can send you. . . . . When I had to set out to go to my king, my *voices* said to me: *Go boldly: when thou comest to the king, he will have a good sign to receive thee, and believe thee.*"

Delafontaine resumed his task. "When the sign came to your king, what reverence did you make it?"

" I knelt and uncovered my head; and I thanked Our Lord, because He had delivered me from the burthen of the churchmen arguing against me there; for they gave up when they knew the sign. An angel on the part of God brought it to the king; and when he and those with him had seen it, and had seen the angel too, I asked my king if he was satisfied. And he said, *yes.* Then I went away into a little chapel near-by, and after my departure, I heard that more than three hundred persons saw the sign. For love of me, and that they should leave off questioning me, God deigned to permit those of my party to see the sign, who did see it."

Here the bishop stopt the interrogatory, well contented, no doubt, with his morning's work.

On Monday, March 12, Jeanne underwent two examinations in prison. Midy and Feuillet again accompanied the bishop as representatives of the assessors, and for witnesses came two doctors of canon-law—Pasquier de Vaux and Thomas Fievé—their first appearance at the trial. There was present also besides the promoter, examiner, notary, and usher, an apostolical secretary, Nicolao de Hubento.

Delafontaine resumed the interrogatory where it had been interrupted on Saturday, and asked if the angel who brought the sign to the king, was the first who appeared to her or another.

" It is always the same, and he never failed me."

" Did he not fail you as to good fortune when you were taken ?"

" I believe, since it pleased Our Lord, that it was better I should be taken."

" Has he not failed you in gifts of grace ?"

" How can he have failed me when he comforts me every day ? St. Katherine and St. Margaret console me too."

" Do you call for them, or do they come without being called ?"

" They come often without calling ; and at other times, if they do not come soon, I pray Our Lord to send them."

" Did you ever call, that they did not come ? "

" I never needed their comfort ever so little, but that I had it !"

" When you made your vow of virginity, did you speak to Our Lord himself ? "

" It was enough to promise it to those sent from him—to St. Katherine and St. Margaret. I made my vow to keep so long as it should please God ; the first time I heard the *voice*, when I was of the age of thirteen."

" Did you never speak of your visions to your curé or any other priest ? "

" No ; only to Robert de Baudricourt and my king. My *voices* did not charge me to conceal them, but I feared lest the Burgundians should hinder my journey, and especially I feared lest my father should prevent my going."

" Was it well to set forth without leave of father or mother ? Is it thus father and mother should be honoured ? "

" They have forgiven me ! "

" Did you not know you were sinning when you left them ? "

" Since God commanded, it was right to do it ! Since God commanded, if I had had a hundred fathers, or a hundred mothers, and if I had been the king's daughter, I must have gone ! "

" When you first saw St. Michael and the angels, did you make them any reverence ? "

" Yes ; and when they were gone, I knelt and kissed the ground where they had rested."

" Were they with you long ?"

" They come often amongst Christians who do not see them. I have seen them many a time !"

" Do not your *voices* call you *Daughter of God, Daughter of the Church, Maid of a Great-heart ?*"

" Before the raising of the siege of Orleans, and since, every day when they speak to me, they have called me *Jeanne the Maid, Daughter of God.*"

" Since you call yourself the daughter of God, why will you not say *Pater Noster ?*"

" I will say it. When I refused before, it was that my lord of Beauvais might confess me."

Here the interrogatory closed for the morning ; perhaps the judge was disconcerted by Jeanne's allusion to himself, in the presence of the three strange witnesses, and had a mind to explain it. He did not preside at the examination in the afternoon. His assistants of the morning came without him, and Delafontaine continued his interrogatory by asking Jeanne about the dreams her father had before she left Domremy.

" While I was still with my father and mother," said she, " my mother told me several times that my father had dreamed that I should go away with the men-at-arms ; and they kept me very strictly, and in great subjection ; and I obeyed them in everything, except in the matter of marriage. My mother told me that she had heard my father say to my brothers : ' If I thought that could happen to Jeanne that I have dreamed, I wish you would drown her ; and if you will not, I will drown her myself.' And he almost lost his senses when I set out to go to Vaucouleurs."

" Did these thoughts or dreams come to your father after you had those visions ?"

" Yes, more than two years after I heard the first *voices*."

" Was it of your own accord or at the request of Robert de Baudricourt you put on your man's dress ?"

" I put it on of myself, and not at the request of any man in the world."

" Did you think you did wrong in putting it on ?"

" No. And *now*, if I were with my own party, and in this dress, I think it would be a very good thing for France, that I should still do as I did before I was taken !"

" How did you propose to deliver the Duke of Orleans ?"

" I meant to capture enough English here to ransom him ; and if I could not capture enough here, I meant to cross the sea with a power to fetch him out of England. . . . My *voices* told me that I should deliver him, and I asked the king to let me deal with the prisoners. . . . If I had continued three years without hindrance, I should have delivered him. . . . My term was less than three years, and more than one—how much more, I cannot now remember."

The interrogator here attempted to re-introduce the subject of the *sign* given to the king. Jeanne curtly replied that she must take counsel with St Katherine, and the examination ended for that day.

The next morning Jean Lemaître, the vice-inquisitor for Rouen, joined the trial of the Maid. The previous day, he had received a formal commission from the grand inquisitor to sit on it as judge to its conclusion. From this command he had no appeal. The Bishop of Beauvais had, at last, dragged to his tribunal an official of the Holy Office, whose presence was all that it had lacked to make it absolutely perfect in the eyes of the orthodox Catholic world. His name would go forth to it, authenticating all the acts of the trial; and except the clergy of Rouen, few or none would ever know under what coercion he had acceded to it. He was a timid, perplexed, irresolute man, but not designedly wicked; for he had for his friend an Augustine monk, Brother Isambard de la Pierre, the most courageous, pious, and pitiful of the very few upright churchmen who acted as assessors.

They went to Jeanne's prison together, and found the bishop already there, with the two Paris doctors, Midy and Feuillet, the apostolical secretary, Delafontaine and Manchon. The vice-inquisitor began his duties by confirming the institution of Jean d'Estivet as promoter in the cause, and Jean Massieu as usher. He then appointed, in the name of the Inquisition, a notary, Nicolas Taquel, and as keeper of the prison, John Berwick. These formalities accomplished, Jeanne was sworn, and Delafontaine, by the bishop's directions, proceeded at once to interrogate her of the sign she had given to the king. She made a hard struggle to keep her secret, and not trespass on the truth.

"Do you wish me to perjure myself?" said she.

The vice-inquisitor took up the word. "Have you sworn and promised to St. Katherine not to tell that sign?"

"I have sworn and promised not to tell that sign. . . . Of myself I swore and promised, because I was too much urged to tell it. And I vow that I will speak of it no more to man!"

What extraordinary pressure was put upon the prisoner here is not shown, but that threats were employed, may be surmised from her subsequent declaration that her judges *condemned* her to speak of that sign; and her next words are a plunge into a figurative narration of the scene in the castle at Chinon, justified to her own conscience probably, by a vein of truth perceptible to her mind, but

quite undiscernible to her interrogators.   To them,
her parable sounded like pure fiction, but they urged
or enticed her on with a multiplicity of questions
and suggestions until they had it all complete.
Here is the sum of what she said :—

"The sign was a crown, and the angel certified
to the king in bringing him the crown that he
should recover all the kingdom of France by God's
aid, and my labour. . . . . This was in the king's
room at the castle of Chinon, after Easter, two
years ago. . . . . The first time I saw the king, he
had the sign. . . . . It was of fine gold, so rich that
I could not count its richness, ... and it signified
that he should hold the kingdom of France. I
neither touched it, nor kissed it. . . . . The angel
came by the command of God, and entered by the
door of the room. . . . . I came with the angel up
the steps to the king's room, and the angel went
in first. . . . . There was a lance-length from the
door to the king. . . . . When the angel came before
the king he bowed, and inclined himself before the
king, and I said : 'My lord, here is your sign ; take
it ;' and the angel reminded him of the beautiful
patience with which he had borne his great tribula-
tions. . . . . He departed by the way he had come.
. . . . I had been constantly in prayer that God
would send the sign to the king, and I was in my
lodging at the house of a good woman near the
castle of Chinon when the angel came, and we

went together to the king. . . . . There were a
number of other angels with him that every one did
not see, and St. Katherine and St. Margaret. I think
the Archbishop of Rheims, the Duke of Alençon,
Charles de Bourbon, and the Sire de la Trémouille
saw the angel. The crown was seen by many
churchmen and others who did not see the angel.
In the little chapel he left me; I was neither glad
nor afraid; but I was very sorrowful, and I wish
he had taken away my soul with him!"

The *secret* that was between Charles and the
Maid, the joy of Charles visible to all the court,
and Jeanne's exalted mood at the time, when her
frequent hallucination of a great light, floating full
of angelic faces, was no doubt before her, may furnish a clue to her parable.

" Was it for any merit of yours that God sent
his angel?" asked the interrogator, pretending to
take the story literally.

" He came for a great cause :—in the hope that
the king would believe the sign; that they would
leave off arguing against me, and let me give succour to the good people of Orleans; and also for
the merit of the king and the Duke of Orleans."

" Why was he sent to you rather than to another?"

" Because it pleased God, by a simple maid, to
drive away the adversaries of the king."

She was asked if before she led the attacks on

Paris, La Charité, and Pont-l'Evèque—her three great failures—she had any revelation from her *voices* bidding her make them. She said, No: the assault on Paris was undertaken at the request of the gentlemen of the army, and that on La Charité by the wish of the king : "and as for that on Pont-l'Evèque," continued she, "after it had been revealed to me at Mélun that I must be taken, I referred nearly everything in the war to the will of the captains,—without telling them, however, that I had a revelation I should be taken."

The next morning, Jeanne was examined again in prison, and the first question was why she tried to escape from the castle of Beaurevoir.

" I had heard that all in Compiègne, from seven years old and upwards, were to be put to the sword, and I preferred to die rather than live after such a destruction of good people. That was one cause. The other was that I knew I had been sold to the English, and I felt that it would be much better to die, than to fall into their hands."

" Did you make the leap by the counsel of your *voices?*"

" No. St. Katherine told me every day not to fly, and God would aid me, and those in Compiègne also. And I said, if God was going to aid those in Compiègne, I would fain be there. But she replied that I must be patient; for I could not be delivered until I had seen the King of the English. I told her that truly I had no desire to see him; for I would rather *die* than be put into the hands of the English! After my fall, I was two or three days that I could not eat or drink, I was so much hurt by the shock. But St. Katherine comforted me, and told me to ask forgiveness of God, and that without fail those in Compiègne should have succour before Martinmas. And then I began to recover, and was soon well."

" In making the leap, did you intend to kill yourself?"

" No. I commended myself to God as I leaped. I thought to escape, and to evade being given up to the English."

" When speech returned to you, did you not curse God and His saints? We have information that you did."

" I have no remembrance that ever I cursed God or His saints, either there or elsewhere."

" Will you refer that to our informations, made or to make?"

" I will refer it to God, and to none other!" Jeanne had not been brought thus far on her way to her end, without discovering that their informations were kneaded with lies.

" Do your *voices* ever ask you for delay before they answer you?"

" St. Katherine answers me at once; but sometimes I cannot hear for the noise of my guards, and the uproar in the prison."

" What requests do you make to your *voices* ?"

" I ask of them three things:—my deliverance ; that God will aid the French, and keep the cities in their obedience; and the salvation of my soul."

The bishop was not present at this interrogatory, and Delafontaine took the opportunity of asking Jeanne why *he*, more than others on her trial, was putting himself in peril.

" He says he is my judge—I do not know that he is. But I bade him be advised not to judge ill; that if he do, and God chastise him for it, I may have done my duty in warning him."

" What is this peril or danger that he risks ?"

" St. Katherine has told me that I shall have succour. I do not know whether it will be to be delivered out of prison, or whether, when I am brought to judgment, some trouble will arise by which I may be released; but I think it must be one or the other. My *voices* tell me most frequently that I shall be delivered with a great victory; and then again, they say to me, *Fret not thyself for thy martyrdom: thou shalt come at last to the kingdom of paradise.* And this they tell me simply and absolutely, and without failing me ever."

" Thy *martyrdom*, Jeanne ?"

" The trouble and adversity I suffer in prison,

that they call *martyrdom;* whether I shall suffer yet greater sorrow, I know not; but I trust God."

" Since your *voices* have told you that you shall come at last to the kingdom of paradise, do you hold yourself assured that you shall be saved, and that you shall not be damned in hell?" interposed Nicole Midy.

" I believe firmly what my *voices* have told me, that I shall be saved, as firmly as if I were in heaven already."

"That reply is of great weight, Jeanne," said the vice-inquisitor.

" I hold it for a great treasure." The poor prisoner, blessed in her ignorance, did not know that to be confident of salvation was to err in the faith; but the perfidious question of Midy had betrayed her into an assertion which constituted one of the twelve articles on which she was condemned to death. The captious, over-subtle, dangerous line of interrogatory was continued; and Jeanne answered readily, all unconscious whether she was being led.

"Do you believe you cannot fall into mortal sin after that revelation?"

"I do not know; but I trust God for all."

"What do you understand by being certain of salvation ?"

" That I keep the vow I have made to God, and guard well my virginity of body and soul."

" Is it necessary for you to confess, since you believe, by the revelation of your *voices*, that you shall be saved ?"

"One cannot too often cleanse one's conscience. I do not know that I have sinned mortally; but I think if I were in mortal sin, St. Katherine and St. Margaret would forsake me."

" To take a man to ransom, and to put him to death a prisoner, was not that a mortal sin ?"

" I never did it." She was reminded of the affair of Franquet d'Arras, and after recounting the matter as it really happened, she added—" I consented to his death if he had deserved it. He confessed himself traitor, murderer, and thief."

" Was it not a mortal sin to assault Paris on a feast day?"

" I do not think it was; but, if it be, it is for God to take cognisance of it, and the priest in my confession to God."

" Was it not a mortal sin to take the Bishop of Senlis's mare ?"

" I firmly believe it was no sin against God. He valued it at two hundred gold crowns, and had the cheque for them. And at all events, I sent it back to the Sire de la Trémouille to be returned to my lord of Senlis. It was good for nothing to ride for me. I did not take it from the bishop, and when I heard that he was discontented at parting with it, I did not wish to keep it. Whether the cheque was ever paid I do not know, nor whether his mare was restored to him: but I think not."

" Was it not a mortal sin to throw yourself from the tower of Beaurevoir ?"

" I did it, not with the intention of destroying myself, but in the hope of saving my body, and that I might go and succour some good people who were in extremity. It was ill done; but I confessed my sin to God, and prayed His mercy, and He pardoned me."

" Were you *very* penitent for it ?"

" I bore a great penance from the hurt I did myself."

" Is it not a mortal sin to wear that male habit you have on ?"

" Since I wear it by the command of God, and in His service, I do not think that I do wrong; and when it shall please Him to bid me lay it by, it will be instantly put off."

The bishop absented himself from the next day's examination, and the vice-inquisitor presided with the same assistants as before. He began by admonishing Jeanne that as to whether she had done anything contrary to the faith, she must refer herself to the judgment of the Church.

" Let my answers be seen and examined by the clergy," replied she. " If they tell me there is anything in them contrary to the Christian faith which

Our Lord taught, I will inquire of my *counsel* about it, and then I will tell you what I have found by my *counsel;* and if there be anything against the Christian faith, I will not uphold it; for I should be very sorry to offend against the faith."

The Church triumphant and the Church militant were declared to her, and the inquisitor required her to submit herself to the determination of the Church militant as to whether what she had said and done was good or evil. Jeanne said she could not, at present, answer otherwise than she had answered already.

She was then sworn, and the interrogatory opened with an inquiry about her attempt to escape from Beaulieu.

" I was never anywhere a prisoner that I would not have gladly escaped. At Beaulieu I had shut up my guards in the tower, when the porter had warning, and caught me. It seems God was not pleased I should escape at that time."

" Have you leave of your *voices* to quit your prison whenever you choose ?"

" I have asked it many times, but I have not received it yet."

" Would you quit your present prison if you saw your opportunity?"

" If I saw the door open, I would go away—*that* would be God's leave to me ! I *firmly* believe that if the door were open, and my guards and the other English not there to hinder me, it *would* be God's leave, and that He would send me succour. Without leave I would not go, unless I made an attempt to *try* whether it might·not please Him that I should escape. It is said, ' Help thyself, and God will help thee.' I tell you this, so that if I *do* go, it may not be said I went without leave." Jeanne's practical sense and audacious candour might have made her judges laugh, had she not betrayed such a pathetic unconsciousness of the peril in which she stood.

The prisoner had renewed her petition to hear mass, which the bishop had rejected at the beginning of her trial, now four weeks past; and in reference to it the vice-inquisitor said—" Since you wish to hear mass, it would be more decent that you should wear a woman's dress. Would you rather put on a woman's dress and hear mass, or keep your man's dress and not hear mass?"

This was a very lively temptation—three months it was and more since she had heard prayers in church.

" Certify me that I shall hear mass if I am in a woman's dress, and on that I will answer you!" cried she.

" I do certify you, that you shall hear mass, but it must be in a woman's dress."

" I answer you. Cause to be made for me a

dress long to the ground, without train, and give it me to go to mass ; and afterwards, when I return here, I will resume the habit I am wearing."

" Should you refuse to take a woman's dress for *always* to go and hear mass ?"

Jeanne could not answer so great a question on the spur of the moment. "I will take *counsel* of that, and then I will tell you," said she. "But pray, for the honour of God and Our Lady, let me hear mass in this city !"

" Then you must wear your woman's dress simply and absolutely."

"Give me a dress like a citizen's daughter, a long coat and a woman's hood, and I will put them on to go and hear mass," urged she, seeing her expectation on the point to vanish. That could not be granted. She pleaded again with tears in her voice : "I entreat you, earnestly as I can,—I beg you, then, to leave me this habit that I wear, and to let me hear mass without changing it ?"

This was utterly refused. She must resume her female dress once for all ; and the dress that had been prepared for her, and offered to her, was the short peasant dress of the girls of Domremy. Amongst her adversaries, Jeanne was not recognised as the glorious martial Maid her king had ennobled, but only as the runaway daughter of a poor labouring couple ; and with the mean spite of malice, triumphing over greatness, they required

her to put on again her primitive garb, that she
might seem to be reduced to her primitive condition. She, poor soul, was so little able to gauge
their wickedness, that when it was proposed to her
first, she fancied that they meant to send her out
in it to beg her bread ; that they wished to degrade
her, not at all that they were seeking to compass
her death. Jeanne would not pretend to despise
her honours. She tried to stipulate for her right—
the long dress of a lady ; or she would be content with the modest dress of a citizen's daughter
—but these only for mass. Her prayer was denied.
The peasant's garb must be worn then, and worn
in prison, or no church-service would be allowed
her. She abandoned her hope, and rejected the
condition. In the castle, in the custody of her
English guards, she said more than once, privately,
that it was safer to wear her male habit than a
woman's dress ; and as for pledging herself to lay
it by for good, that, in no case, could she do without the leave of God.

The vice-inquisitor left that matter, and asked
her again : " Will you not, on what you have said
and done, submit yourself to the judgment of the
Church ?"

" All my words and works are in the hand of
God, and I submit myself to Him," replied she.
" And I assure you that I would neither do nor
say anything against the Christian faith by our

Lord established ; and if the clergy say that I have upon me any act or deed contrary to it, I will not sustain it, but will thrust it from me. I cannot answer you otherwise now, but on Saturday, send the notary to me, and with God's help, I will answer him, and it shall be put in writing."

Delafontaine now took up the interrogatory again, and questioned her to satiety about her visions and *voices*. Amongst other things, he asked if she always did what her *voices* bade her do.

" I accomplish the command of God, made to me by my *voices*, with all my might, as far as I understand it."

" Did you ever in the war do anything without their leave ?"

" You have been answered of that—read your register, and you will find it. However, the feat of arms before Paris was made at the request of the soldiers, and the assault on La Charité at the request of my king, and they were neither *by* nor *against* the command of my *voices*."

" Did you ever do anything contrary to their will and command ?".

" What I could do, and knew how to do, I have done to the best of my power. And as for my leap from the donjon of Beaurevoir, which I made against their command, I could not help it. And when they saw my necessity, and that I could not help it, they saved my life, and hindered me from killing myself. Whatever I have had to do in great affairs, they have always succoured me :—that is a sign they are good spirits. . . . . St. Michael, when he came to me, told me St. Katherine and St. Margaret would be sent to me, and that I was to act by their counsel ; they were ordered to guide and advise me in what I had to do, and I was to believe what they said to me, and that it was by the command of God."

"What doctrine did St. Michael teach you ?"

"The first time I heard him I was a child, and was afraid. Since, then, he has taught and shown me so much that I believe firmly the angel was he. Above everything, he told me that I must be good, and that God would help me ; and he recounted to me the pity there was in the kingdom of France. The greater part of what he taught me is in *this* Book." *This Book* must have been the Book of the Holy Gospels on which the prisoner was sworn, and which probably, at the moment, still lay under her hand.

"Do you think it is a great sin to act against the command of St. Katherine and St. Margaret who appear to you ?"

"Yes, for one who can do better. The most I ever grieved them was when I leaped from the donjon of Beaurevoir, for which I cried their mercy."

"Will they take corporal vengeance for your offence ?"

" I do not know—I never asked them."

"You have said that *for telling truth men have sometimes been hanged*—if you knew in yourself any crime or fault for which you ought to die, would you confess it ?"

" No." This closed the Thursday's examination. Friday was a rest day.

On Saturday morning, as soon as Jeanne had made her oath, she was bidden to describe the form, stature, fashion, and clothing of St. Michael when he appeared to her.

" He was in the form of a very true, good man," replied she, and then added with emphasis: " I believe the words of St. Michael, who appeared to me, as firmly as I believe that our Lord Jesus Christ suffered death and passion for us ; and what moves me to believe it is, the good counsel and comfort I have had of him, and the good doctrine he has taught me."

The examiner quitted that theme, and asked again would she submit all her words and deeds to holy mother Church to determine whether they were good or evil. She answered him :

" As for the Church, I love it, and would support it with all my might, for our Christian faith; it is not *me* whom you should vex, and keep from going to church to hear mass ! As for my advent, and the good works I have done, I must refer my-

self to the King of Heaven who sent me, and to
Charles, son of Charles, King of France, who shall
be King of France."

She was urged again: "*Say* if you will submit
yourself to the judgment of the Church."

"I submit myself to God who sent me, to Our
Lady, and to all the blessed saints in Paradise.
Our Lord and the Church are one. It seems to
me that you ought not to make a difficulty about
it. Why do you make a difficulty, as if they were
not one?"

Delafontaine perceived that the Maid did not
understand the dogma of *The Church* as taught by
Rome. She had got hold of a rank heresy—that
heresy, so-called, which was, by and by, to release
half Christendom from the papal thrall. She had
got hold of it in its primitive, practical form, and
she held it fast. Her love and fear of God, and
her utter dependence on Him, had taught her the
true faith which sustained her through her long
martyrdom, and never left her comfortless. The interrogator set himself to instruct her in that vital
article of Roman theology, *Unam Sanctam Ecclesiam,*＊ but to very little purpose. Her work was appointed her of God, the strength to do it was given

---

＊ "That Christ has established a Church upon earth; and that
this Church is that which holds communion with the see of Rome,
being one, holy, Catholic and apostolical.

"That men are obliged to hear this Church; and therefore, that

her of Him; He was her only hope and consola-
tion in the midst of her enemies. Her mind cut
clear through all sophistications. To refer it to the
determination of the Church whether she had done
ill or well in what she had done for France, was to
refer it to the determination of the churchmen who
were trying her. They were her adversaries, and
had already condemned what she had done. To
their judgment, she would not submit it.

Delafontaine pursued his explanation : " There
is," said he, " the Church triumphant, where is God,
the saints, the angels, and the souls of the saved.
And there is the Church militant, which is our holy
father the Pope, vicar of God on earth, the cardinals, the prelates, the clergy, and all good Christians and Catholics ; which Church, well assembled,
cannot err, and is governed by the Holy Spirit—
will you submit to this Church militant ? "

Jeanne was very sure that the churchmen before
her, with the Bishop of Beauvais presiding, could
err, and grievously, and wilfully, and wickedly, and
she reiterated her former answer : " I came to the
King of France on the part of God and the victorious Church above, and to that Church I submit

she is infallible, by the guidance of Almighty God, in her decisions
regarding the faith.

" That St. Peter, by divine commission, was appointed the head
of this Church, under Christ its founder ; and that the Pope or
Bishop of Rome, as successor to St. Peter, has always been, and
is at present, by divine right, head of this Church."

all my good deeds, and all that I have done or shall do."

"And what say you now to that woman's dress we have offered you to go and hear mass?"

"As for a woman's dress, I will not yet put it on—not until it shall please God. And if I am brought to death, and I must be unclothed to die, I beg of you, my lords of the Church, that you will have the charity to allow me a woman's long shift, and a kerchief on my head. . . . . For I will rather die than revoke what God has caused me to do; but I believe firmly that He will never let me be brought so low, but that I shall have His help, and by miracle!"

"Since you say you wear your man's dress by God's command, why do you ask for a woman's shift at death?"

"I shall be satisfied if it be long," replied Jeanne.

Her judges did not warn her that if she were brought to death, the *fire* would be her terrible fate, and no garment would save her modesty there. They went on to remind her that she had said, early in her trial, that if she were permitted to depart, she would take a woman's dress, and they asked her whether that would be pleasing to God.

"If you let me go in a woman's dress, I should soon put on a man's to do what my Lord has bidden me. Not for anything would I make oath not to dress and arm myself to do the pleasure of God!" was her resolute answer.

" Do St. Katherine and St. Margaret hate the English?" inquired Delafontaine, his question suggested by her vehemence.

" They love what our Lord loves, and hate what God hates!"

" Then does God hate the English?"

" Of God's love or hate for the English, or what He will do to their souls, I know nothing; but I know well that they shall be all thrust out of France, except those who shall die there!"

" Was God for the English when they were in prosperity in France?"

" I do not know that God hated the French; but I believe He might let them be chastised for their sins."

" What guarantee and help do you look to have from God for wearing your man's dress?"

" For that, as for all else I have done, I have never desired to have other wage than the salvation of my soul."

" What were the arms you offered at Saint-Dénis?"

" A suit of white armour and a sword. I offered them for devotion, as is the custom of soldiers when they have been wounded; and because I had been wounded before Paris, I offered them at Saint-Dénis, which is the cry of France."

In the afternoon there was a second examination, and it being the last the bishop intended to subject Jeanne to before her new confessions and assertions were given to the assessors, he came to the prison, accompanied by the vice-inquisitor, and the six counsellors from the University. The only witnesses were Brother Isambard de la Pierre, and her chief gaoler, John Grey.

The examiner began on the subject of her Standard, and after several questions about the angels painted on it, he asked:

" Did you inquire of your *voices* whether, by virtue of your Standard, you would win all the battles you fought ? "

" The *voices* told me to take the Standard on the part of God, and to carry it boldly, and God would help me," replied she.

"Was your hope of victory founded on your Standard or on yourself?"

" It was founded on God, and on none other."

" Has it not been revealed to you that if you lost your virginity, you would lose your good luck, and that your *voices* would come to you no more ?"

" That has not been revealed to me."

" Do you think that if you were married, your *voices* would not come to you ?"

" I do not know; I leave it to God."

" Do you believe your king did well to kill, or cause to be killed, the lord Duke of Burgundy?"

" It was a great pity for the kingdom of France; but whatever there was between them, God sent me to the succour of the King of France."

" Why did you like to look at your ring on which *Jhesus Maria* was written, when you went out on any expedition."

" For love and honour of my father and mother who gave it me; and because, having it on my hand, I touched St. Katherine, who appears to me."

" When you hung garlands on the tree of your village, were they offerings to those who appear to you ?"

" No."

" When your saints come, do you revere them by kneeling and bowing ?"

" Yes, I revere them as much as I can; for I know that they are they who are in the kingdom of paradise."

" Do you know anything of those persons who are deluded away by the fairies ?"

" I have heard them spoken of, and that they go on the Thursday; but I do not believe it, and I think it is sorcery."

" There are many questions that you have not yet answered: should you be bound to speak more fully before our holy father, the Pope, than you have done before my lord of Beauvais and his clerks?"

"I demand to be taken before him! Before *him* I will answer all that I ought to answer."

This appeal to the superior power was good; but it might as well have been made to the winds. The bishop and his accomplices took care, also, that it should be suppressed when the XII. Articles came to be composed for Jeanne's condemnation. The examiner passed to other matters, and asked if she had not waved her Standard over the head of her king.

" Not that I know of," said she.

" Why was it carried into the church at Rheims at the coronation, rather than those of the other captains ?"

"It had been in the travail—reason good that it should be at the triumph ! "

With this brave answer, the judges and counsellors made an end of interrogating the Maid, and left her.

On the morrow, Sunday, March 18th, a council was held at the bishop's house, at which were present the inquisitor, the six counsellors from the University, the Abbot of Feçamp, the Prior of Longueville, Nicolas Venderez, Raoul Roussel, Delafontaine, and Coppequesne. The bishop explained how Jeanne had been privately examined during the past week, and the advice of these select assessors on what remained to be done in the trial was required by the judges. The council proceeded to review the work of the doctors, who, since the close of the public interrogatory, had been busy collecting and arranging the chief avowals of the accused, and, before separating, agreed to turn over the books of canon-law to see what they contained relative to the matter in hand.

The following Thursday there was held a second council, attended by twenty-two assessors. What had been further compiled by the leading counsellors in the interim was read. Each assessor spoke in turn; and after a long and warm debate, it was concluded that the whole must be reduced to a certain number of propositions or charges, that all vice of procedure might be avoided. On these charges it was proposed to examine Jeanne again, and in public, before moving further.

Few as were the assessors at this council in comparison with those at the earlier interrogatories, they were numerous enough to furnish many diversities of opinion about the prisoner. One thought it highly improbable that she would have preserved her chastity if she had been destitute of other virtues; a second saw nothing impossible in her revelations; a third was inclined to believe her inspired. Some declared that the questions proposed to her were over subtle and difficult for her to answer by herself; some that the imputations of

magic and sorcery had not been sustained ; some
that it was impossible to repute her a heretic on
anything shown against her yet, except her refusal
of submission to the Church.   This was, however,
enough to condemn her, and was doubtless the opportunity by which the astute bishop had foreseen,
from the beginning, that he should be able to take
her.   Jeanne had made her inspiration her law.   To
that had been sacrificed—first, love to her father
and mother, then honour to her king, and now was
to follow the grand and last struggle against the
authority of the Church.

Concerning Jeanne's disobedience, there were
various scandals afloat in Rouen.   It was ru-
moured that certain soldiers, feigning themselves
prisoners of Charles's party, had been secretly
introduced into her prison, to warn her beforehand
against submitting to the Church, assuring her that
if she did, her enemies would assume authority
over her as her judges.   Loiselleur was pointed
at as the chief traitor.   The notary Boisguillaume
knew that he advised Jeanne not to believe or
trust the ecclesiastics who were trying her, assuring
her, if she did, she would find herself deceived,—
which was very true and just advice, whatever
malicious intention it concealed.   But, in fact,
Jeanne's refusal of submission to the Church appears to have been, in the first instance, the spon-
taneous expression of her belief that the voice of

God in her soul was a law with which no earthly
power had a right to interfere. Her varying replies,
as she was variously instructed and advised afterwards, prove that her mind worked independently
both of those who wished to mislead and of those
who wished to save her, and that in the midst of
the confusion they created, she kept her own faith
distinct, as the only faith to be relied on, not to
fail her at the last. If, with her lips, in one bitter
passage of trial, she seemed to disavow it, in her
heart she disavowed it never.

Before drawing up the articles which were to
assume the form of an Act of Accusation against
Jeanne, it was necessary to verify the register of
her examinations; and on the Saturday morning it
was read over to her in prison by Manchon—present the inquisitor, and five of the University counsellors, Beaupère, Morrice, Midy, Feuillet, and De
Courcelles. The promoter and Delafontaine were
also there, and a stranger, an official from the ecclesiastical court of Coutances. The promoter offered
to prove the truth of any matter in the register
Jeanne might wish to deny, and she was sworn to
add nothing to her former assertions unless it were
true. She then desired Manchon to read question
and answer straight forward, saying, that what she
did not contradict, might be held as affirmed.
When the lecture was concluded, she declared it to
be correct, and the only matter on which she

wished to add anything was her habit. Where she
said :

" Give me a woman's dress to go home to my
mother, and I will accept it," she explained that it
was only to be out of prison, and when she was out,
she meant to seek counsel what she ought to do.

Before the doctors left her, she made a new petition, urgent and pathetic, that she might be suffered
to hear mass the next day, which was Palm Sunday, and also that she might have the sacrament
of confession, and the Eucharist at Easter. In consequence, the bishop visited her the following morning, accompanied by the promoter, Beaupère, De
Courcelles, Midy, and Morrice, to speak to her
about the conditions on which alone her prayer
could be granted. She must resume the peasant
dress she had been accustomed to wear in her
birthplace.

Jeanne pleaded to have the comforts of her religion as she was. The bishop said she should have
them willingly, but not unless she resumed the
attire of her sex.

" My *counsel* does not advise me to do it—I cannot do it yet," she said.

" Will you consult the two saints who appear to
you ?" proposed the bishop.

" At least, let me hear mass without changing
my habit," persisted she. " The changing it does
not depend on me."

The four Paris counsellors then united their voices, praising her piety and devotion, and entreated her to put herself in the way of satisfying them.

" If it depended on me, it would soon be done," was her sad answer.

" Will you consult your *voices* as to whether you may change it, to have the Eucharist at Easter?" urgèd the bishop again.

" I cannot change it—not even to receive my Saviour! Let me hear mass to-day as I am. My habit is no burthen on my soul—to wear it is not against the Church."

The bishop only gave her the same reply as before; and the promoter added this to the sum of her heinous crimes, that she preferred to keep on her male dress to hearing mass, and that she had refused to communicate at Easter, as the Church enjoins on all true and faithful Catholics to do.

Jeanne had repeatedly entreated since the opening of her trial, that she might be removed from the castle into the ecclesiastical prison. Properly guarded there, she might, perhaps, have submitted on this point; though she had the opinion of the clergy of her own party, with Gerson at the head of them, that she committed no sin in wearing a soldier's dress, having regard to her motives; and though she believed she had still work to do for

God and the King, and for France, which would make wearing it as necessary as ever. But in the ecclesiastical prison, she would not have been exposed to those indignities which made her obstinate—and it was essential to the success of the bishop's beautiful trial that she should appear as obstinate and perverse as ill-usage could make her; there, also, she would have been secured from those base manœuvres which the men who were contriving her death had finally to resort to, to accomplish it. Many of the assessors reprobated her detention in the castle, and many reprobated the decision of the bishop not to allow her the sacraments at Easter, except on condition of changing her dress; but he could afford to bear their blame, with the University doctors and the English council to support him, and Jeanne gained nothing by the little advocacy exerted in her favour.

V.

THE ACT OF ACCUSATION.

O N the Monday in Passion Week, March the 26th, a select council met at the bishop's house to hear read the Act of Accusation, drawn up from the register of the notaries, and from the informations that had formed the basis of the interrogatories, which the promoter in the trial meant to bring against the Maid. At this council were present, besides the two judges, and six counsellors from Paris, only Venderez, Delafontaine, Loiselleur, Châtillon, and Andrew Marguerie, archdeacon of Rouen. They agreed that the charges were well composed, and that upon them Jeanne should be finally examined and heard. The next day was appointed to begin the reading of them before her for that purpose, and citations to attend in the hall where

the public sessions had been held, were sent to
the assessors.

They assembled to the number of thirty-eight.
The hall was crowded with the people of the
English court, the Earl of Warwick conspicuous
amongst them, keeping a jealous eye on any members of the tribunal who betrayed a desire to help
or enlighten the accused.

As soon as Jeanne had been brought in, and
conducted to her place, the promoter rose, and
addressed a requisition to the judges, that they
would cause her to answer to each of the charges
he was about to prefer against her; and that in
case she refused to answer, she should be reputed
contumacious, and excommunicate for manifest
offence. He further required that if a term of
delay were granted her to answer on any charge,
if not answered when the term expired, it should
be taken for true and confessed, as law, use,
and common custom demanded. His address
ended, he delivered in his bill of articles, making oath that neither for fear nor for favour, neither
for malice nor hatred, but only in zeal for the faith,
did he bring the charges contained in it against the
prisoner.

The judges required each of the assessors to
give his opinion on the promoter's requisition, and
after some debate, they spoke in turn, agreeing
that the charges should be read to the accused,

and that she must swear to answer truly on matters of fact; on matters of doubt and difficulty all were for granting her delay, and a few said, before proceeding to excommunication, give her at least three delays.

The bishop then admonished Jeanne in his honied, specious way, that the ecclesiastics before whom she stood were men expert in divine and human law, who intended with all clemency and compassion to proceed against her, not vindictively desiring the punishment of her body, but her instruction and reduction into the way of truth and salvation. And as she was not sufficiently wise and learned to answer by herself in such difficult and arduous questions, he proposed that she should choose one or more of those on the consistory as her counsel; or, if she declined all the doctors present, he would offer her others, providing that on matters of fact she would answer in her own person, and swear to speak the truth.

Jeanne had either been apprized, or it had forced itself upon her mind, at last, that her life was in question; but it was with a brave, composed resolution that she answered her artful persecutor. " First, as to what you admonish me for my good, I thank you, and all the company. As to the counsel you offer me, I thank you too, but I have no intention of departing from the counsel of God. As to the oath you require of me, I will swear to tell you the truth in all that concerns your trial;" and so she knelt down, laid her hand on the Gospels, and made her oath.

The bishop's offer of counsel was too tardy to save Jeanne from making the confident assertions and indiscreet avowals by which she had become fast entangled in his snares ; but it sounded well to the assessors, not initiated into his secrets. His plausibility did not, however, delude Jeanne. More probably than not, he had anticipated her refusal, which was calculated to bias the court against her, and to be interpreted as a sign of the overweening self-confidence and pride which were alledged as the roots of her enormities. But, in fact, no counsel that she could rely on had yet discovered himself to her on the consistory. Fabry and Châtillon were not able to hold their own against the judge, and where was the profit of an adviser who could be browbeaten into silence? Brother Isambard de la Pierre, who was better to be trusted, had only appeared, thus far, as a silent witness at her examinations in prison. He came in late on this occasion, and finding no place on the tribunal, went and sat down near her, and during the course of the morning, was detected by the Earl of Warwick trying by signs and gestures to help her. She discerned a true man in *him*, and, at the opportunity, seized his advice without hesitation, and spoke on it ; but it did not serve her—no advice *could*

serve her against the league united for her destruction.

The promoter did not read the Act of Accusation
himself. The bishop deputed Thomas de Courcelles
to the task. It consisted of seventy charges, which
occupied two days in the repetition. In the pre-
amble, Jeanne was qualified as a sorceress, divina-
tress, pseudo-prophetess, invocatress of demons: as
given to ·magic arts: as superstitious, schismatic,
idolatrous, sacrilegious, malicious: as an apostate, a
blasphemer of God and His saints: as scandalous,
seditious: as a disturber of the peace, cruel, inciting
to war and bloodshed: as defiant of the decencies of
her sex in assuming the arms and habit of a man:
as a prevaricator and seducer of the people in con-
senting that they should adore her: as a usurper
of divine honours, and a heretic.

Jeanne listened with grave, amazed indignation
as these horrible epithets were hurled at her in the
sonorous tones of the young and eloquent De Courcelles. He put zeal enough into his work ; and
there they stood facing each other: so strangely
defiant ; the two, who in their generation served
France the best ; she to deliver it from the English
yoke ; he to deliver it from the Papal despotism.

To each charge as he read it, and paused, Jeanne
answered promptly: for the most part with a simple
denial, and a referring of the accusation to God.
When she confessed to a matter of fact, she fre-

quently added, that for the construction put upon
it, she referred that also to God. When any article
affirmed what she had declared to be untrue in her
previous examinations, she only said, "I have already answered you otherwise of that." Although
the purity of her life had been certified to the bishop,
and was well known to his counsellors—although
none had yet ventured to impugn it to her face,
into the Act of Accusation were introduced several articles implying the reverse, and the charges
of magic and sorcery which it maintained, could
only accord with dissolute behaviour. But she was
not tortured into any long defences or explana-
tions. Not a word of recrimination passed her lips,
nor any inquiry as to who were the persons of her
own party that had witnessed against her to her
enemies:—who had given up copies of her correspon-
dence with the Count of Armagnac ; who had told
of her gazing at her *Jhesus Maria* ring when she
went out to fight ; who had furnished descriptions
of her attire when she left Vaucouleurs, and of the
rich raiment she wore when she was the victorious
Maid the king had delighted to honour ; who had
travestied her encouraging talk to her soldiers ;
who had shown in a baleful light the simple ways
of her village home ; and who had frankly lied
about her. The doctors who worked at drawing
up the propositions, put the bad colouring on
many innocent events and circumstances, and were

responsible for keeping out of view all Jeanne had
said that went towards her clearance ; but the testimony they began upon, and which had been the
ground-plan of her examinations, had all the appearance of testimony voluntarily contributed by
traitors in the obedience of Charles VII. A more
loyal and generous soul never breathed than Jeanne ;
for though many a sore thought of neglect and betrayal must have ached in her heart, she showed
no trace of them ; nor afforded her adversaries a
moment of such triumph as they would have felt,
had she evinced a knowledge that her king, or any
of her party, had failed her, or played her false.

The first article in the Act of Accusation concerned Jeanne's refusal of submission to the Church.
She replied to it much as before: "I believe that
our holy father, the Pope of Rome, the bishops
and other churchmen, are to guard the Christian
faith, and to punish those who offend against it ;
but as for me and my deeds, I will submit them
only to the Church in Heaven, to God, the Virgin
Mary, and the saints in Paradise. And I firmly
believe that I have not failed in the Christian faith,
nor would I fail."

The second charge was of sorcery, divination, and
magic arts, which Jeanne denied, and of usurping
divine honours, to which she said: "If the people
kissed my hands and clothes, it was not by my
wish, and I did my best to keep me from it."

In the fourth, the legendary fairies of Domremy had become the Maid's familiar spirits, and her decent kindred, ignorant old women who instructed her in anything but what was good. She answered: " As to fairies, I do not know what they are ; as to my bringing up, I was duly taught my belief, and learnt it as a good child ought."

In the fifth and sixth, the Beautiful May and the fountain were described as the haunts of evil spirits, and Jeanne was said to have frequented them alone and at night ; to have made incantations there, and to have hung up garlands on the branches of the tree, which in the morning were gone.

In the seventh, she was accused of keeping mandragora in her bosom, hoping to have prosperous fortunes thereby.

In the eighth, her flight with her parents to Neufchâteau had been turned into leaving home without their permission, when she was not sixteen years old, and taking service in an inn kept by a hostess, called *La Rousse,* where lived many incontinent women and soldiers ; where she led the horses to water, and performed many other tasks which young girls were not used to perform ; where also she learned to ride, and to use arms.

In the ninth, the disappointed lover who cited her before the ecclesiastical court at Toul for her refusal to marry him, had become a lover who re-

fused to marry her, because of her consorting with
the company at La Rousse's house.

In the eleventh, the audacious, laughing speech
she had made to Robert de Baudricourt of the
three sons she should have when her work for God
was done, was charged on her as an impious boast,
which the governor was said to have recounted
before prelates and nobles, and all manner of great
people.

The twelfth and thirteenth treated of her assumption of the male habit ; of her pompous clothing—
precious cloth of gold and rich furs ; of her wearing
not only the short tunic and ordinary garments of
the other sex, but of her putting on the tabard and
toga ; of her capture before Compiègne clad in
a splendid *huque* of scarlet cloth of gold; and of
her wearing her hair trimmed round in the style
of a man ; all of which it declared to be dissolute
and detestable, and against the Holy Scriptures
and holy canons.

Having denounced her iniquity in this matter in
strong terms and at some length, Thomas de Courcelles asked if she professed that God had commanded her to put on a dress which, in His own
Word, was declared to be a thing abominable for a
woman to do.

" I have answered you enough of that," said
Jeanne.

He then inquired if she would resume her natural habit that she might receive the Eucharist at Easter.

" No," replied she, " I will not yet put off this dress, either to receive my Saviour or for any other thing. It makes no difference to me in what dress I receive my Saviour, and you ought not to refuse me because of it." Being urged again as to the command or revelation in obedience to which she put it on, she exclaimed, in a tone of vext impatience : " I know well why I put it on, but I do not know how to reveal it ! " Some more of the counsellers begged her to lay it by to hear mass. " No, I will not yet," she answered firmly. " It does not depend on me when I shall lay it by. And if my judges refuse to let me hear mass, Our Lord can make me hear it, when it shall please Him, without them."

The seventeenth article charged her with boasting of a divine mission to the king. She answered with spirit and energy : " I did bring news on the part of God to my king :—that Our Lord would restore to him his kingdom, crown him at Rheims, and drive out his adversaries. And in this I was the messenger of God. I did bid him set me boldly to work, and I would raise the siege of Orleans. I did say that all the people should be reduced to his obedience, my lord of Burgundy with the rest, and that if they would not make submission, he should compel them to it by force."

The eighteenth charged her with refusing peace, and inciting to bloodshed. She answered nobly : "As for peace with the Duke of Burgundy, I besought him by letters and by ambassadors, that there might be peace. As for the English, the only peace for them is, that they be gone into their own country, into England!"

The twenty-first accused her of presumption and pride in addressing her famous summons to Henry VI. and the regent. " I did not send it in pride and presumption, but by the command of God ; and if the English had believed my letters they had been wise, as they shall see before seven years are out ! "

The twenty-fifth denounced her as cruel in war. " First, I demanded of the enemy if they would make peace, and when they would not make peace, I was quite ready to fight." Charged with using enchantment to secure victory, she said : " In whatever I have done there was neither sorcery nor any other bad art. As for the good luck of my Standard, its luck was the luck God sent it."

Soon after this article had been read the court rose for that day, and after dinner Brother Isambard de la Pierre, Jean Delafontaine, and Martin l'Advenu, a Dominican friar, went to the castle by leave of the inquisitor, to try if they could persuade Jeanne to submit to the Church. They explained the dogma to her in its widest sense, instructing her that she had a right of appeal to the Church Universal ; but Loiselleur who had now, in his character as priest, ventured to assume the rôle of her *director*, had taught her before that it meant, practically, submission to the ecclesiastics trying her. And her confidence in him was not shaken. Brother Isambard and his associates sought honestly to help her, and on the morrow, when the business of reading the Act of Accusation was continued, the good Augustine monk went again late, and took a seat close by her below the tribunal.

Jeanne appears to have come before her judges on this second morning despondent and exhausted. Article after article was read up to the fiftieth, and she replied to them no more than : " I refer you to my former answers—for the conclusion I refer myself to God." Asked with regard to one charge, if she believed she did well to assault Paris, she said bravely : " The gentlemen of France wished it, and for my part, I think they did their duty in going against their adversaries."

The fiftieth article, and the tenor of two or three preceding it, provoked her to speak defensively; for they struck at the root of her trust in God, affirming that when she asked counsel of her *voices*, she invoked demons to her aid.

" I have answered you of that," said she. " To believe in my revelations, I want no advice of bishop or curé, or any other. I believe firmly,—

as firmly as I believe that our Lord Jesus Christ
has suffered death to redeem us from the pains of
hell,—that the angels who appear to me, and
speak to me, are St. Michael, St. Katherine, and
St. Margaret, sent by God to counsel and comfort me ; and while I live, I will call them to my
succour !"

"In what manner do you call upon them?"
asked Thomas de Courcelles.

"I pray to God and Our Lady that they will
send me counsel and comfort, and then they send
them."

"And in what words do you pray ?"

Jeanne recited her secret prayer to God before
the crowded court.

*Very tender God, in honour of your holy passion, I
pray you, if you love me, that you will reveal to me
how I ought to answer these churchmen. I know
well, as to this habit, the commandment why I took
it, but I do not know in what manner I ought to leave
it off. Be pleased therefore to teach me.*

"And very soon they come," added she. "I
have often news by my *voices* of *you*,"—looking up
at the bishop.

"What do they say of me ?" asked he.

"I will tell you it apart. Three times to-day
I have heard them, and St. Katherine and St.
Margaret have told me how to answer about my
dress."

Thomas de Courcelles proceeded with his reading of the articles. The fifty-third alleged that against the precept of God and the saints, Jeanne had proudly and presumptuously assumed dominion over men, constituting herself head of an army of sixteen thousand soldiers, amongst whom were princes, barons, and many other nobles, who all fought under her, as under a chief of war. "If I was chief of war, it was to beat the English!" cried the Maid.

The fifty-fourth charged her with leaving her father's house at seventeen years of age, and of since living amongst men, as was never heard of a woman of devout and modest behaviour. "My government was of men," said she, "but in my lodgings and in my chamber I had always a woman with me, and in the camp I lay down to sleep dressed and armed."

The fifty-fifth accused her of perverting the revelations she professed to have from God, to the acquisition of worldly wealth and honours for herself and family, after the ways of the false prophets.

The fifty-sixth, on the authority of Katherine of Rochelle, speaking before the ecclesiastical court in Paris, affirmed that Jeanne had boasted of having two Counsellors of the Fountain, who would come to her after she was taken. Katherine had also offered it as her opinion, that unless Jeanne were well kept, she would get out of prison by the

help of the devil. This woman was the solitary
witness whose name was revealed by the Maid's
persecutors—a worthy specimen of the sources of
their information against her.

The sixtieth charged her with refusing to swear
unconditionally, in contempt of the precept of the
Church, and with telling her judges they should not
know everything she knew. "As for the counsels
of my king, because they do not concern this trial,
I have refused to reveal them," said she. "As for
the sign given to the king, I told it, because I was
condemned to tell it."

The sixty-first detailed her refusals of submission
to the Church militant. "As for the Church militant,"
said she, "I would bear it all the honour and reverence in my power. But as for referring my acts to
the determination of that Church militant, I must
refer them to God, who caused me to do them."

There was some clamour in the hall at this bold
utterance, and Brother Isambard, who appreciated
the danger into which she was rushing far better
than she could do, made a brave effort for her
rescue. Her demand to be taken before the Pope
had been easily passed by in her prison, but there
were now many witnesses, and leaning over to her,
he said with energy: "Appeal to the Council of
Bâle."

"Who speaks there? Hold your peace, in the
devil's name!" cried a voice from the tribunal. It

was the Bishop of Beauvais who had been surprised into the unseemly adjuration.

There arose loud tumult and contention, in the midst of which the prisoner asked her prompter, "What is the Council of Bâle?"

"It is a congregation of the Universal Christian Church, where there are as many clergy of your party as of the English—appeal to be brought before it," urged the good monk, disregarding the enraged judge.

"Oh, if there are any of my party there, I will refer myself to it," replied Jeanne, and raising her voice, she exclaimed, "*I appeal to the Council of Bâle!*"

Manchon, the notary, put his pen to the register to record the appeal. The bishop stopt him. There was no need to write it; he disallowed the appeal. The accused had no right of appeal from the tribunal of her Ordinary. Manchon held his hand: Boisguillaume also.

"Ah!" cried Jeanne, looking at them reproachfully: "what makes against me, that you write; what would make for me, that you leave out!"

The confusion increased both amongst audience and assessors. The Maid's enemies feared for a few minutes that she was going to escape out of their toils. Some on the tribunal thought the appeal valid. The inquisitor's friend had suggested it to the accused. But the inquisitor was a poor perplexed coward, and did not support him; while the bishop was bold, bad, and defiant. He rallied from his momentary panic, silenced the doubtful assessors, and called the court to order. Thomas de Courcelles then continued his lecture of the articles, as if the accused had never spoken.

She made no response to any charge afterwards, beyond the formal words referring the promoter to her past assertions, until the last was concluded, when she said with dignity: " The crimes that are charged against me, I have not done. For the rest I submit myself to God; and I do not think I have done any thing against the Christian faith."

The bishop put the final interrogatory. " If you *had* done anything against the Christian faith, would you submit yourself upon it to the Church, and to those to whom the correction of it belongs ?"

" Grant me a delay until Saturday after dinner, and I will answer you," replied she.

She was then re-conducted to her prison, and the court was dismissed.

Brother Isambard's interference to rescue the Maid did not pass unrebuked. The Earl of War-wick, meeting him in the castle-yard, asked how he dared to prompt her, and threatened to have him tossed into the Seine. The bishop also, surprised at Jeanne's sudden yielding to the monk's counsel, thought it could not be the first time he had spoken

to her, and he inquired of John Grey, *who* had
received admittance into her prison the previous
day.   The gaoler told him his own clerk, Jean Delafontaine, had been there, with two monks, Brother Isambard de la Pierre and Brother Martin
L'Advenu; and he indulged in such angry menaces
against them, that the inquisitor plucked up spirit
enough to declare he would sit no more on the
tribunal if any harm befell them.   Delafontaine
was, however, either so alarmed, or so assured that
his superior meant foul play such as he would not
share, that he left Rouen, and his name disappears
entirely from the list of counsellors after this public session on the 28th of March.

On the Saturday, Easter-eve, the two judges,
the six counsellors from Paris, and William Hayton, an English priest, who had been present at the
interrogatories in the hall, but not in the prison,
went to Jeanne to receive her answer to the article
on which she had asked delay—submission to the
Church.

The formal demand was addressed to her, " Will
you submit to the judgment of the Church which
is on earth all you have done or said, whether it be
good or evil, and especially the crimes and iniquities which are laid against you, and all that concerns your trial ?"

Whether Loiselleur had been with Jeanne to
advise her during the interim does not appear ; but

her reply sounds much more as if she had worked it out for herself, with thought and prayer, than as if it had been suggested to her. She said, " I will submit to the Church militant, provided that it will not command me to do anything impossible. And what I repute impossible is, that I should be required to revoke the things which I have said or done, declared in the trial, my visions and revelations, and my works on the part of God. What Our Lord commanded, or shall command me to do, I will not revoke for any man that lives. It would be impossible for me to revoke them. And if the Church should desire to make me do anything contrary to what God has bidden me, I will not for anything obey."

" But if the Church militant tells you that your revelations are illusions, or diabolical things, or superstitions, or evil things, will you not submit yourself to the judgment of the Church upon them ?"

" I will submit myself to the judgment of God, whose bidding I will always do. I know well that what is contained in my trial came to me by His commandment; and what I have affirmed to be done by the commandment of God, it would be impossible for me to deny. And if the Church militant ordered me to do so, I would not refer it to any man in the world, but to God only, whether I have not always done His good commandment."

" But do you not believe that you are subject to the Church which is on earth—that is, to our holy father thė Pope, the cardinals, archbishops, bishops, and other prelates of the Church ?"

" Yes, *God first served.*"

" Have you a command from your *voices* not to submit yourself to the Church militant ?"

" I do not answer anything I take into my head ! What I answer is by the command of my *counsel,* and it does not command that I shall *not* obey the Church, *Our Lord first served.*"

The doctors left questioning her. This reply was tantamount to a refusal of obedience, and would serve the purpose of the bishop and his accomplices admirably. Just judges, faithful, upright servants of the Church they professed to serve, would have noted, at once, that it was honest instruction in its dogmas Jeanne needed, not punishment for her imperfect conception of them, and they would have stood betwixt her and her adversaries, thirsting for her innocent blood. But they were not just judges or faithful servants: they were, some wolves, and some dumb dogs afraid to bark, and the poor prisoner was wise in refusing to exchange her trust in God who comforted her every day, for refuge in a fold tended by such shepherds and such guardians.

Before quitting the prison, the bishop asked her whether, at Beaurevoir, Arras, or elsewhere, she had ever had any *files* in her possession : nothing he dreaded so much as her escape.

"If any have been found upon me, I have nothing to answer you," replied Jeanne; and the churchmen left her, and went their way.

VI.

THE TWELVE ARTICLES.

ON Easter Monday and the two subsequent days, the judges and their chief counsellors met at the bishop's house, and proceeded to extract from the seventy propositions comprised in the Act of Accusation, what they called *the doctrine* of Jeanne, and to reduce it briefly into XII. Latin Articles for the purpose of transmission to consultants, as the practice of the Inquisition was in cases of heresy.

No notary was present, and Nicole Midy drew out the first draught of the articles. Another counsellor, not named, proposed fifteen corrections, and Jacques Texier defaced the original draught of the articles with so many marginal notes and interlineations that it was almost illegible. Ultimately a copy was produced in which five of the corrections were made in the precise terms suggested ; six were made with some modification, and four were rejected.

There is an air of guilty consciousness about the compilation of these famous, or *infamous* XII. Articles. The council that devised them is the only council during the trial—the only reunion of the doctors for any purpose—of which, in the definitive edition, done into Latin by Thomas de Courcelles, the names of the members are not recorded. The articles were not affirmed by Jeanne, nor even read to her. But Manchon was set to work to write out fair copies, which were sent to the University of Paris, to the Chapter of Rouen, to the bishops of Avranches, Lisieux, and Coutances, and to a great number of ecclesiastics besides, some assessors and some not, with a requisition from the judges that they would give in, under their hand and seal, by a certain date, their opinion on what the articles contained contrary to the orthodox faith, the Holy Scriptures, the Roman Catholic Church, the holy canons, and public morals.

Manchon, who had written down every word that fell from Jeanne's lips had better reason than almost any other to know how false the XII. Articles were; but he made some fifty or sixty copies of them, and authenticated them with his signature, pleading to himself that he dared not contradict the opinion of such great and learned men as the Bishop of Beauvais and his clerks. And so they went forth

to the world, to condemn Jeanne, and to sink her
memory for many years ; but to be themselves, in
turn, condemned as " unfaithful, wicked, calumnious, fraudulent, and malicious."

They were all this, but they lied with a most
specious resemblance to the truth. The prepara-
tory informations were quite put aside, and out
of her own mouth she was made to supply all that
was necessary to destroy her. Her good words,
her pleas, her qualifications were suppressed, and
what was ill-sounding without them was put forward bare. When the Chapter of Rouen met to
deliberate on receiving the articles, they were so
puzzled between what they read, and what they had
many of them heard during the public interrogatories, that they agreed to defer their opinion until they
knew what the University of Paris pronounced on
them. At the same time they declared that first,
and before all, they ought to be well explained to
the accused, and accompanied with a charitable admonition to submit herself to the Church.

Meanwhile Jeanne had fallen sick in prison.
Easter-day was for her a day of fasting and humiliation, a day of solitude and tears, and each day
that dragged after it grew heavier with sorrow.
She had in her heart the peace that passes understanding, but her body languished for sweet air
and sweet sun. The gray walls of her prison

seemed to grow darker and closer every morning, the weight of the chains upon her limbs seemed to grow deader every night. And as if these were not enough, the bishop ordered her to be confined with another when she lay down on her bed, so that she could not stir, and had no ease, sleeping or waking. Her English guards were the only persons she saw— chosen base fellows who hated her, and were afraid of her ; who wished her anywhere out of the world, so that their task of keeping her were ended. Now, with the connivance of their superiors—baser than they—they diverted their dulness by mocking her, teasing her, terrifying her ; and when she forgot her miseries in slumber, they roused her, and told her she was going to be killed. Abstemious to asceticism as she had been, here she endured hunger and thirst, and all the mean indignities mean men could inflict on a proud, pure, devout woman, left at their mercy. She reproached them sometimes, weeping at their inhumanity, but they only laughed her to scorn.

Her vigorous young frame and brave spirit could not bear up beyond a certain point. April was budding in the woods and fields : the new life of spring was swelling through the dry veins of nature. A feverish languor and weariness came over her, a heavy burthen of pain. Sleep and appetite left her. At first, those about her thought she was feigning, and they left her to suffer on ; but suddenly their eyes were opened with great alarm, and they saw that if she had not care and tendance she might die, and escape her *reparation.*

The bishop sent her a carp from his table to tempt her to eat, and she did eat a little, and fancied it made her worse.   Jean d'Estivet went to see her, taking with him one of the Paris physicians, Jacques Tiphaine.   They found her lying unclothed, visibly a sick and suffering girl, but with chains upon her limbs still notwithstanding her weakness. Tiphaine asked her where her pain was, and felt her side and her pulse, and Jeanne told him about the carp, implying, poor soul, that the bishop had meant to poison her.   Nothing farther from his thoughts ! His kindness was spent upon her that she might live to endure the fire.   D'Estivet forgot *that* for a moment, and angrily took up his patron's cause, abusing her, and calling her vile names.   Jeanne was passionately grieved, and cried and raved again in her fever, and grew so much worse that War-wick forbade him her room, and called into counsel two more physicians, Guillaume Desjardins and Guillaume de la Chambre.

Before Guillaume de la Chambre went into the prison, Warwick took him aside, and told him the king would not for anything Jeanne should die, *unless by justice;* he had paid for her dearly enough, and expected to have her burned.   "Therefore," added he, "attend her with solicitude, and make her well if you can."

When the doctors had seen her, and had consulted together, they told the earl that it was necessary to bleed her.

"Bleed her!" cried he. "That is very hazard-
ous. She is cunning, and might kill herself after."

Perhaps they thought it would be a happy thing
for her if she could slip quietly out of life. They
had nothing else to suggest, and Warwick, at
length, consented to the experiment, and Jeanne
was bled. It did not relieve her of all her pain,
and the weakness that ensued, she thought, must be
surely the coming on of death. She entreated that
she might have the sacraments, and word was
carried to the bishop. Immediately he went to
see her, with Nicole Midy and several other priests,
announcing when he entered her prison, that he
came to comfort her in her sickness, and that his
visit was one of charity. And then he proceeded to
make it one of business also. Three monitions or
warnings were always given by the Inquisition to
its victims, and to economise precious time, the
bishop made use of this opportunity to give her the
first. He informed her with solemn tediousness
that a great number of good and learned men had
been consulted on her errors, and that they condemned them, desiring she might be well instructed
for the salvation of her body and soul, and well
warned of the grave peril to which she exposed
herself by refusing to return to the way of truth

and obedience. He also offered to send her daily
wise and virtuous persons to confer with her, and
teach her.

Jeanne heard him patiently to the end, thanked
him for what he said of her health, and then passing over his exhortation and offer of counsel, she
said, " It seems to me from what I suffer that I am
in great danger of death ; and if it please God thus
to deal with me, I pray you to let me have confession and my Saviour also, and burial in holy
ground."

The bishop replied, " If you desire to have the
rites and sacraments of the Church, you must do
as a good Catholic ought to do, and submit yourself
to the Church."

" I cannot answer you anything on that now, but
what I have answered before."

" The more you fear for your life because of your
sickness, the more you ought to amend your life.
You will not, cannot have the sacraments of the
Church as a Catholic, unless you submit to the
Church."

Jeanne contented herself with replying, " If my
body die in prison, I hope you will let it be buried
in holy ground. If you do not, I leave it to God."

" You once said in your trial that if you had
done anything against the Christian faith, by Our
Lord established, you would not maintain it. You
tell us you have had many revelations on the part

of God by St. Michael, St. Katherine, and St. Margaret ; if some good Christian came affirming to have had a revelation from God concerning you, would you believe it ?"

"There is no Christian in the world who could come and tell me of having had revelations that I should not know whether it was true or not ; and I should know it by St. Katherine and St. Margaret."

"Do you imagine that God cannot reveal anything that it shall not be known to you ?"

"Surely He can. But I would believe neither man nor woman without a sign."

"Do you believe that the Holy Scriptures are revealed by God ?"

"You know I do ! It is good to know they are."

Upon this she was summoned, exhorted, begged to take the good counsel of the priests and scholars there present, and to believe that too, for the salvation of her soul. And then she was asked again— *would* she submit to the Church.

"Whatever may become of me, I will neither say nor do otherwise than I have said before in my trial," replied she.

The priests tried her again one after the other, Jacques Texier, Gerard Feuillet, and three more, and she answered them not a word. Then Nicole Midy took up his text, and told her how St. Matthew in his Gospel wrote :—

If thy brother shall trespass against thee, go and

tell him his fault between him and thee alone: if he shall hear thee, thou hast gained thy brother. But if he will not hear thee, then take with thee one or two more, that in the mouths of two or three witnesses every word may be established. And if he shall ne-glect to hear them, tell it unto the Church: but if he neglect to hear the Church, let him be unto thee as a heathen man and a publican.

And then the preacher expounded the words, and concluded by assuring the poor sick girl that unless she would submit to the Church, the Church would cut her off, like a heathen woman and a Saracen.

"Nay," said Jeanne, "I am a Christian! I was baptized, and I shall die a Christian."

Perhaps she looked in her weakness and weariness like dying before their eyes; for another of the priests said: "Jeanne, you have asked for your Saviour; we will promise to give you your Saviour if you will submit to the Church."

"Of that submission I will not answer otherwise than I have done. I love God, and serve Him; I am a Christian, and holy Church I would aid and maintain with all my might."

"Shall we make a beautiful procession and prayers that you may be reduced to a good con-dition, if you are not in one?"

"Yes. Fain would I that the Church and all good Catholics should pray for me!"

With that answer the bishop and his assistants left her.

This monition was made to Jeanne on the 18th of April. By that time copies of the XII. Articles had been transmitted to all the consultants, and their opinions were beginning to come in. Sixteen doctors and six bachelors of divinity had met in the archiepiscopal chapel on the 12th, and had deliberated together. Nicole Midy and his fellow-counsellors from Paris were all there; Jean Fabri, Hûlot de Châtillon, and Brother Isambard were there, and so was Nicolas Loiselleur. The great University doctors were an authoritative group. If any amongst the clergy or monks of Rouen doubted the articles, or felt an impression contrary to them, he was put to silence; general impressions were not wanted, but particular opinions on those particular articles, the verity of which the bishop's chief clerks and confidants, who compiled them, were ready to vouch for. An opinion was finally agreed on in common, and written out to this effect :—That Jeanne's revelations were lies or delusions of the devil; and that there appeared in her divinations, superstitions, scandalous and irreligious acts, rash and presumptuous words, blasphemies, things contrary to the love of our neighbour, a sort of idolatry, schismatic principles, and errors in the faith. No other conclusions could, in fact, be drawn from the XII. Articles, such as they were.

Brother Isambard consented to this opinion with the rest, and sure in his own mind that Jeanne would be condemned, unless she could be rescued from her judges at Rouen, and sent either to Rome or Bâle, he set off to Avranches, to consult the bishop, a very old and learned divine, concerning appeals and submission to the Church. The bishop referred him to a passage in the writings of St. Thomas, and the monk found the opinion of that great authority to be that: " In things doubtful that touch the faith, recourse should be had always to the Pope or the General Council." The aged prelate declared himself to be of the same opinion as St. Thomas, and expressed much dissatisfaction at what Brother Isambard told him respecting the denial of Jeanne's appeals. For his written opinion on the XII. Articles he forwarded to the judges St. Thomas's dictum. The promoter cursed him roundly for it, and it was suppressed.

D'Estivet was better satisfied with the others, which were an almost unanimous chorus of condemnation. A few diversities and difficulties appeared amongst them, but none that were too hard to be removed or evaded. The Abbots of Jumièges and Cormeille advised that all the trial, and not the XII. Articles only, should be sent to the University of Paris to have its opinion on so diffi-

cult an affair. Raoul Sauvage strongly denounced
the *doctrine* contained in the articles, which he supposed to have been affirmed by the accused, (as did
probably most of the consultants;) but he urged that,
considering the fragility of her sex, they ought to be
repeated to her, with instruction not to presume so
much on her revelations; and finally, that they should
be sent to the Pope with the qualifications they
merited. Eleven lawyers of Rouen who consulted
together, were oracularly indecisive : they thought
Jeanne should be excommunicated for wearing a
male dress—unless she was commanded by God
to act as she had done; and that she broke the
article of the faith, *Unam Sanctam Ecclesiam*, in
refusing to submit to the Church,—if her revelations did not come from God, which was not to be
presumed. Three bachelors of divinity living in
Rouen, Pierre Minier, Jean Pigache, and Richard
Grouchet, chose to deliberate apart from the
twenty - two theologians who had met in the
archiepiscopal chapel, and they agreed that : if the
revelations of the accused were lies or works of
the devil, most of the propositions on which they
were consulted were suspect in the faith, and contrary to good morals ; but if they came from God,
which did not appear certain, it would not be permitted to interpret them in bad part. ·

To counterbalance these hesitating opinions, there
were a few very furious. The Bishop of Coutances,

addressing himself to the Bishop of Beauvais only, and quite ignoring the vice-inquisitor in the cause, declared Jeanne's *doctrine* to be so heretical that even if she abjured, she must not the less be kept in safe custody; and Denis Gastinel, a bachelor of civil and canon law, said this custody ought to be for life, on bread and water.

As soon as all the provincial opinions had come in, Nicole Midy, Jean Beaupère, and Jacques Texier, were despatched to Paris with letters of credit from the judges and the English council, and copies of the XII. Articles—but *not* of the interrogatories—to receive the opinion of the University. Very sure what that opinion would be, the bishop, in the absence of the three doctors, went on with the monitions yet due to the accused.

The springs of life in the young are deep and strong. Health had returned to Jeanne, and on the 2d of May she was brought from her prison into the hall to receive her second warning in public. The bishop had issued numerous citations to the clergy of Rouen and its vicinity, and seventy or more had answered his summons, the Chapter of the cathedral amongst them. Before the prisoner appeared, the bishop addressed the consistory, telling them how long and patiently she had been entreated to mend her life, and return to the true and saving way; and how, sustained by the malice and

subtlety of the devil, she still persisted in her iniquities, notwithstanding all that had been done.
When she was led to her place in front of the
tribunal, he proceeded to exhort her to hearken to
the counsel which was about to be given her for
her body and soul, apprizing her that if she did
not act upon it wisely, her peril would be very
imminent.

The bishop, throughout the trial, systematically
put forward his colleagues of highest reputation ;
and with a fine show of fairness, Hûlot de Châtillon, who had endeavoured to help and screen the
accused before, was now deputed to admonish her.
Loiselleur had not spared to counsel Jeanne in the
interim since the last monition, and whether she
had hearkened to him or not, there was reason
to anticipate that the present would prove a very
disastrous scene for her. She came before the consistory evidently with her mind made up. She
looked wan, weary, and despondent, but obstinate.
She had been told, or she had evolved the certainty
from her own consciousness, that submission to the
Church would entail the necessity of allowing that
she was either a shameless liar, or that it was not
God but the devil who had sent her to the succour
of the king. And such an avowal she was stead-
fastly purposed her adversaries should not extort
from her, though she died for it. The bishop bade
Châtillon instruct her with tenderness, and then

the archdeacon stood forth, and holding in his hand a schedule of her errors in particular, he proceeded to deliver himself first of a general admonition on them.

He signified to her the opinions of the consultants on her *doctrine*, and told her every true Christian was bound to obey the Church as a mother. He then said she sinned in wearing a male habit, in refusing to quit it to communicate at Easter, and especially in attributing her conduct to the counsel of God and His saints. He next enlarged on her allegory of the sign given to the king, calling it a *lie;* and then, ascribing her revelations to the demon, passed under review, in that aspect, all her other errors. Finally, he entered into a wordy dissertation on the Church militant, and concluded by saying, "God has given to the clergy the power and authority to judge of men's actions, whether they are good or bad; the Catholic Church can never err, can unjustly judge none, and whoever pretends the contrary is a heretic." He then asked Jeanne if she would correct and amend her ways by his advice.

"Read your book, and then I will answer you," said she, indicating the schedule the archdeacon held. "I trust God, my creator, for all; I love Him with all my heart!"

"Have you nothing more to answer to my general admonition?"

"I trust my Judge for it; he is the King of heaven and earth," was her response.

Châtillon could only proceed to his particular admonitions. "You formerly proposed that your words and deeds should be reviewed by the clergy, as they have been reviewed,—what answer you now to the commands of the Church?"

"I believe in the Church, and that it cannot err; but as for my words and deeds, I will submit them to God, my creator, in His own person, who made me to do them."

"Do you mean to say you have no judge on earth? Is not our holy father the Pope your judge?"

Jeanne's nerve was shaken, though her resolution was firm. Her memory had grown confused amongst her many advisers. She did not call to mind her former appeal to the Pope in the presence of this great assembly, or say a word by which the perplexed Châtillon could understand she believed him to be equivocating with her; but feeling herself baited, misled, purposely deceived by some one or other of her instructors, she exclaimed with passionate impetuosity, "I have a good master in God, and to Him I will submit, and to none other!"

A fatal word for her! The Chapter of Rouen had heard it with their own ears, and need doubt the articles, and delay their opinion no longer. Everything was going perfectly for the bishop, and taking the worst possible course for her. Châtillon, though honest and well-meaning enough, was undiscerning, harsh, and without tact. He began to threaten her, which only roused her temper, and made her defiant.

"If you will not believe the Church and the article *Unam ecclesiam sanctam catholicam* you will be a heretic, and by the sentence of other judges, you will be punished by being burnt!"

Jeanne had learned now that the fire might be her doom, and she was not startled. "I will say no more," she repeated. "If I saw the fire I would still say what I have said, and nothing else."

"If the General Council were here, would you submit to that?"

"You shall draw nothing more from me."

"Will you submit to our holy father the Pope?"

"Take me to him, and I will answer him." And otherwise she would not speak.

Châtillon left that subject for the present, and expatiated on her next great sin—her male dress. She answered him with decision: "As I have said before, I will gladly put on a long dress and a woman's hood to go to church, and receive my Saviour, providing that directly after, I may lay it by, and take again that I now wear."

She was told it was unnecessary for her to wear it any longer, especially being in prison. "When

I have done that for which God sent me, then I will return to my woman's dress," said she.

After more vain expostulations, the archdeacon went on to her *voices* and visions, and reasoning of her parable of the sign given to the king, as the pure fiction he supposed it to be, challenged her to refer the truth of it to some of the princes and nobles whom she named as witnesses of it. This drew the net closer round her than ever. She dared not boldly appeal to them, and still less could she bear to refuse to appeal to them. Men of her party had betrayed her already. She did not know who was false or who faithful. After her long, her total abandonment, she could not be assured that there was *one*, from the king downwards, true to her; *one* who would stand by her, and declare that her story had a veiled meaning, and that these judges in the pay of Charles's adversaries, were knavish dastards for trying by threats to make her disloyal, and to wrest his counsels from her lips. And above all, she had that counsel, and the secret between him and her, still to guard. She found her refuge in evasions, all hurtful to her cause; evasions that gave a triumph to her persecutors, and made the bishop more venturesome at every step.

"Will you refer to the Archbishop of Rheims? to Marshal de Boussac, to La Hire, to Charles de Bourbon? Will you refer to any others of your side, who may send us word under their seals what the truth of that sign is?" asked he.

"Send a messenger, and let me write to them about all this trial!" was her response, and she would make no other.

"If we grant a safe-conduct for two, or three, or four knights of your party to come to Rouen, will you submit to them the truth of the apparitions named in your trial?"

"Let them come, and then I will answer you."

"Will you submit yourself to the Church of Poitiers, where you were examined?"

No; Jeanne would put her trust no more in man. "Do you think to take me in that way, and draw me to you?" said she. Little wonder she despised their reference, and saw a trap in it.

Why had not some of those priests of Poitiers, and Orleans, and Tours, instead of making barefoot processions about their churches, put on their shoes, and made a pilgrimage into Normandy, to speak a word for the poor prisoner, whom they had held to be a good Christian and a good Catholic, and whom their king's enemies had given such long and loud warning they meant to burn for a witch and a heretic?

The baseness of those who forsook Jeanne, glares out almost more hideously than the baseness of the basest of those who destroyed her. But that France, in her fallen estate, bore *her*, one might

think heart and conscience were dead throughout
the whole nation !

Châtillon and others spent themselves in argu-
ments and entreaties that she would yield and submit to the Church, and then the bishop took up
the word, and said—" If you do not submit to
the Church, the Church will abandon you. And if
the Church abandon you, you will be in great peril
of body and of soul. You will risk incurring the
pains of eternal fire as to your soul, and of temporal fire as to your body, and by the sentence
of other judges."

Jeanne looked up at him white, defiant, prophe-
tic. " You will not do to me what you say, but
evil will catch *you*, body and soul!" cried she.

" Will you tell us a reason why you will not submit to the Church ?" asked a well-meaning doctor,
persuasively.

She would not answer. Divines, canon lawyers,
civil lawyers, ecclesiastics of all ages and all sorts,
plied her, and pleaded with her till they were all
weary together. She would not speak a word. At
last the bishop, interposing, said—" You have been
well warned, Jeanne ; you had better re-consider
yourself."

" Within what time am I to re-consider myself?"
she inquired.

" At once, and answer if you will."

She would not. The consistory began to disperse, and she was conducted back to her prison. Two days after, the Chapter of Rouen, without waiting any longer for the return of the doctors from Paris, gave in their opinion on the XII. Articles; adding to it, that for her persistent obstinacy, it appeared to them that the accused ought to be judged a heretic.

Jeanne received her third monition on the 9th of May—only the second anniversary of her return to the king after the glorious raising of the siege of Orleans. She seemed almost to have lost her memory of days and hours; but she must have remembered that triumphant meeting with Charles, when he looked so glad that the people thought he would have kissed her.

Massieu came to her in the morning with a grave face enough, and being freed from her chains, he and John Grey conducted her into a chamber of the great tower, where she had never been before— into the torture-chamber. There were assembled the bishop, the inquisitor, Venderez, Loiselleur, Châtillon, Erard, the Abbot of Saint - Cormeille of Compiègne, Hayton, Marguerie, and another ecclesiastic named Morel. Mauger Parmentier, an apparitor of the Inquisition, was also there, with his brother-tormentor, and the rack was ready for service.

When Jeanne was brought in, the bishop began

to tell her that, on certain points of her trial, it was necessary to have a true answer from her own lips. He had positive information that she had lied on some, and most vehement presumptions that she had lied on others. The tormentors were present, and had their instruments prepared; and unless she would answer the questions about to be put to her, they would, in obedience to his orders, reduce her to speak by torture.

Jeanne defied him to his face. "If you make them tear me limb from limb, and drive my soul out of my body, I will tell you nothing more!" cried she, fiercely. "Or, if I do tell you anything, afterwards I will always say that you dragged it from me by force!"

The bishop moderated his tone of menace, and asked her if she had heard her *voices*, or taken counsel with them lately. She said she had, and particularly on the day following her admonition in the hall.

"They comforted me on Holy Cross day—I think it was St. Gabriel who came: my *voices* told me it was. I begged their counsel whether I ought to submit to the Church, since I am so hard-pressed, and they answered me, that if I would have God aid me, I must in everything trust God. He has always been master of my acts; the Enemy has had no part in them at all."

. "Have you asked your *voices* whether you will be *burnt ?*"

"Yes, I have asked them whether I shall be burnt, and they say, if I trust Our Saviour, He will help me."

"Of the sign of the crown you gave to the king, will you refer the truth of *that* to the Archbishop of Rheims ?"

" Let him come here, and let me hear him speak, and then I will answer you.   He will not dare to say the contrary of what I have said."

The bishop was proceeding with the interrogatory, and pressing some unbecoming question on Jeanne, when Hûlot de Châtillon, touched by her brave spirit and simple piety, and perplexed in his own mind almost past bearing, broke out, and said she ought not to have such an inquiry proposed to her, and she was not bound to answer it.   The bishop and his congenial assistants were angry at his interruption, and some very high words arose. Châtillon, much more indignant than alarmed, declared that, in his opinion, a trial carried on in this sort was entirely null.   The prelate, forgetting his dignity in his rage, bade the archdeacon hold his tongue, and let him speak.   He then ordered Jeanne to be taken back to her prison, saying that her obstinacy was so excessive, he feared it would do no good to put her to the torture, and before applying it, he would take further counsel.

Three days later, he called a council of twelve assessors at his own house, to deliberate on its expediency. Nine out of the twelve gave their voices against it. The three who voted for it were Loiselleur, who said it would be for the good of her soul; Morel, who wished to know the truth about her lies; and Thomas de Courcelles, who arrived at the council after a useless visit to Jeanne, to persuade her to submit to the Church. The vice-inquisitor spoke when the rest had finished, and said she must be tried again, and asked if she did not believe she *ought* to submit to the Church; and the proposal of the bishop to put her to the torture was negatived.

Jean Beaupère and Nicole Midy returned from Paris, leaving Jacques Texier behind, and on the 19th of May the judges convoked their assessors to meet in the chapel of the archiepiscopal palace, to hear read the opinions of the University on the XII. Articles. Fifty or more ecclesiastics assembled.

The bishop opened the council with an exposition of how he had received the advice of numerous doctors and masters upon the confessions and assertions of Jeanne, and that they were now met to deliberate on what further remained to be done in the cause. Touching what had been already done, he ordered to be read a letter from the Uni-

versity to the king, expressing its satisfaction there-
with, to this tenor:—

" *To the very excellent, very high, and very power-*
ful prince, the King of France and England,
our very dread and sovereign lord.

" Very excellent prince, our very dread and sovereign lord and father, your royal excellence, above
everything, ought to be careful to keep the honour,
reverence, and glory of the Divine Majesty, and His
holy faith, in extirpating errors. . . . . In continuing
to do this, your royal highness, in all your affairs,
will find aid and prosperity. . . . . Your noble magnificence, by sovereign mercy, has begun a very good
work for our holy faith; that is, the judicial trial
against the woman called *the Maid*, ... of which
we have learnt the procedure by the letters sent
us, and by the relation of our very honoured and
very reverend supports, the masters Jean Beaupère,
Jacques Texier, and Nicole Midy. . . . . And
truly, that relation heard and considered, it seems
to us that the trial of this woman has been held
with great gravity, with holy and just method,
which ought to satisfy every one. And we humbly
return thanks for all these things, first to your
sovereign majesty, then to your very high nobility,
and lastly to all those who have bestowed their
pains, labour, and diligence on the matter. . . . .
After several convocations and deliberations

amongst ourselves, ... we send your excellence
our opinions and conclusions on the articles laid
before us; . . . . and if anything remain to be
said about them on our part, the reverend masters
returning to you, who have been present at our
deliberations, can fully declare it. . . . . And may
it please your magnificence to believe them; for,
verily, they have worked with much diligence and
pious affection, and without sparing their pains or
persons, or taking heed to the notorious perils of
the journey; . . . . and by their learning and prudence the matter has been, and please God will be,
conducted to the end wisely, holily, and reasonably.
. . . . Finally, we pray your highness that it
may by justice, be briefly finished; . . . . for the
length and delay are very perilous, and it is necessary that notable and great reparation be made;
that the people who have been much scandalised
by this woman, may be reduced to good and holy
doctrine and belief. All to the exaltation of our
faith, and to the praise of the eternal Divinity:
who, we pray, may keep your excellence in grace
and prosperity to glory everlasting.

" Written at Paris in our solemn congregation,
celebrated at Saint-Bernard, the xiiii. day of the
month of May ccccxxxi.

" Your very humble daughter,
" THE UNIVERSITY OF PARIS."

If there were present any assessor whose conscience irked him for giving a condemnatory opinion on the XII. Articles, without requiring to
compare them with the register of the interrogatory, he might take comfort, on learning from
this atrocious letter, that the great University of
Paris herself had been perfectly contented to deliberate on them; to view the trial with one eye
blindfolded, after the manner of a partisan, and so
to see her way straight to the judgment she had
pronounced before the trial began. The whole
body of Manchon's notes would have been excessively embarrassing to discuss with that object to
compass; and when Beaupère, Midy, and Texier
set off to Paris without them, they were no doubt
well assured that their learned brethren, who domi-
nated the cabals of the University, would compla-
cently overlook an omission that abridged their
difficulties: though upright men, intending to do
just judgment, might have denounced it as an im-
pudent snare to catch them in error.

The University forwarded by the doctors a second
letter to the Bishop of Beauvais, commending him
as a zealous pastor of the Church. This also was
read to the assembly. Then came a narrative of
the manner in which the Faculties of divinity and
law had held their deliberations in Paris; and finally,
the result of these deliberations. The theologians
pronounced their condemnation of each of the

XII. Articles in a distinct form. The lawyers pronounced, with an air of caution for the accused and for themselves, that *if* she had asserted the propositions contained in the articles, and *if* she affirmed them, being in sound mind, she was schismatic, apostate, a liar, and accursed; and if she refused to obey the Church after admonition, the competent judge ought to abandon her to the secular power, to receive a punishment proportioned to her crimes. The University, as a body, adopted these opinions, and the letters despatched with them to the king and the Bishop of Beauvais, expressed very frankly what conclusion would alone satisfy her leading spirits.

When all these documents had been read and consulted over, the judges required the assessors present to give one after another their sentences upon the Maid.

Nicolas Venderez, the bishop's chaplain, speaking first, said—"Let the cause be concluded at once; let the sentence be given, and let her be relinquished to secular justice." Only Midy and Marguerie followed this lead.

The Abbot of Feçamp, speaking next, said— "Let the promoter ask her if she has anything more to say; let her be *again* admonished, and this done, unless she will return to the way of truth, she is a heretic; and let sentence be given, and let her be relinquished to secular justice." Thirty-four of the assessors agreed to this.

Guillaume Boucher, a divine of Rouen, said— "Let her be charitably admonished again ; let the XII. Articles, and the decision of the University on them, be read to her ; and if she will not obey, then proceed forward." The Prior of Longueville, Pierre Morrice, and Jean Pinchon gave sentence to the same effect.

Jean Beaupère adopted the opinions of the University of Paris, as did the majority of the assessors, but the final conclusion of the affair he desired to leave to the judges. Raoul Sauvage, Pierre Minier, Brother Isambard de la Pierre, and Pierre Houdenc also declined the responsibility of condemning her to death. By the letter of the law, she was a heretic. But she was a minor, only just nineteen, and if the judges would, they could place her under instruction till she came to maturer understanding.

The judges, however, accepted the sentence of the Abbot of Feçamp, and his numerous following. They assigned Jeanne a day to receive the further warning all but three of the assessors had voted for, and deputed one of the doctors from Paris, Pierre Morrice, to give it on the following Wednesday, May the 23d.

Events were now hurrying on to a conclusion. The Duke of Bedford got away out of Rouen

with his wife, leaving the Cardinal-bishop of
Winchester to see their crime well accomplished,
and numerous false French, for whom it had an
interest, came in to witness the end.   One day,
Jeanne was surprised in her prison by a visit from
Jean of Luxembourg, his brother, the Bishop of
Thourenne, and Haimond de Macy, her lively acquaintance at Beaurevoir.   The Earl of Warwick
and Lord Stafford brought them in.

There was more purpose than mere cruel curiosity
in this visit.   Jeanne had been so nobly loyal to her
king, her party, and herself, that her trial would be
a failure, save as regarded her personal destruction,
unless she could be surprised or tempted into some
weakness and betrayal.   It was impossible for her
ecclesiastical foes to hold out to her any false hopes
or promises of deliverance ; for inquisitorial law
could offer her but one of two alternatives—submission to the Church, or death by fire.   But there
was nothing, either within or without, to hinder a
man like Jean of Luxembourg from dangling a
bait before her eyes, and lying to any extent to
persuade her to take it.

He addressed her with a serious air, and said—
"Jeanne, I am come to treat for your ransom, if you
will promise never more to bear arms against us."

She looked up at him, and replied—"You are
mocking me.   You have neither the will nor the
power."

The Burgundian lord repeated his words, with
an assurance that he really meant what he said ;
but Jeanne only shook her head, and answered
again—" Nay, you have neither the will nor the
power !"   And when he still persisted, she glanced
at Warwick and Stafford, and exclaimed, with a
flash of her former fire—" You have neither the
will nor the power !   I know these English will kill
me, thinking after my death to recover all the
kingdom of France ; but were there here a hundred
thousand *goddams* more than there are, yet should
they *never* have this kingdom !"

Stafford was so enraged at her words and look
that he would have struck her, but Warwick caught
his arm.

It was a day or two after this, that Massieu came
to conduct her into a room of the castle near her
prison, where she found assembled the two judges,
the promoter, the Bishops of Thourenne and
Noyon, and seven of the assessors, Châtillon,
Beaupère, Midy, Erard, Morrice, Marguerie, and
Venderez.

After a few preliminary words from the bishop,
Pierre Morrice gave Jeanne the solemn monition
on which the assessors had agreed her fate must
depend.   The style in which he did it was not calculated to save her.   He began by addressing to
her, in the form of reproaches, the XII. Articles
which professed to summarise her doctrine, and

the opinions of the University doctors upon them ;
verbally abbreviating some, and not retaining all
their substance, and never once pausing to give
her the opportunity of challenging, denying, or
renouncing any : thus—

I. First, thou, Jeanne, dost say, that at the age
of thirteen or thereabouts, thou hadst apparitions
and revelations of angels, of St. Katherine and
St. Margaret, whom thou didst frequently see with
thy bodily eyes ; that they talked with thee, and
told thee many things, fully declared in thy trial.

On this point, the scholars of the University of
Paris and others say, that considering the manner
of these apparitions, the matter of the revelations,
and thy person, that they are feigned, lying, seductive, and pernicious ; or else that they proceed
from malign spirits and devils, Belial, Satan, and
Beelzebub.

II. Thou dost say that thy king had a sign to
know thee sent of God : that St. Michael, with a
multitude of angels, some of whom had wings
and some crowns, and amongst whom were St.
Katherine and St. Margaret, came to thee in the
town of Chinon, and went with thee up the steps
of the castle into thy king's chamber ; before whom
the angel bowed himself, and then offered him a
crown. Once thou didst say, when thy king had
this sign, he was alone ; another time, that the
crown which thou dost call a *sign* was given to the

Archbishop of Rheims, who gave it to thy king, in the presence of many princes and nobles whom thou dost name.

As to this point, the scholars say, it has no likeness to truth, but is rather a presumptuous, seductive, pernicious lie, and derogatory to the dignity of angels.

III. Thou dost say that thou knowest St. Michael and the angels by the good counsel and comfort they give thee; because they name themselves to thee, and the saints salute thee; that thou dost believe it is St. Michael who appears to thee, and that his words are good, as firmly as thou dost believe the faith of Christ.

To this the scholars say, that the signs stated are not enough whereby to know angels and saints; that thou dost believe too lightly, and affirm with temerity. And as to the comparison, thou dost err in the faith.

IV. Thou dost say that thou art certain many things yet in the future will come to pass; thou dost boast of having discerned hidden things by revelation; and of having recognised men whom thou hadst not seen before, and this by the *voices* St. Katherine and St. Margaret.

Of this the scholars say, it is superstitious divination, presumptuous fable, and foolish boasting.

V. Thou dost say that by command of God, and to please Him, thou didst put on and continuest to

wear a male habit; that thou hast God's command
to wear a short tunic, jacket, hose fastened with
many tags, thy hair cut round above thy ears, and
nothing by which thy feminine sex can be discerned
save what nature forces on thee. In this dress thou
hast often received the sacrament of the Eucharist;
and though frequently admonished to leave it off,
thou dost refuse, saying sometimes thou wouldst
rather die, and at other times, "unless it were by
God's command;" and that if thou wert with others
of thy party in it, it would be a very good thing for
France; thou dost also say, that not for anything
wilt thou swear not to dress and arm thyself thus,
and that in all this thou dost act well, and by the
command of God.

As to this point, the scholars say, that thou dost
blaspheme God, and despise Him in His sacraments;
that thou dost transgress the Divine law, Holy Scrip-
ture, and canonical rule; that thou dost err in the
faith, and art full of boasting; that thou mayst be
held as suspected of idolatry, and as having given
thy person to the devil, imitating the rites of the
heathen.

VI. Thou dost say that thou hast caused to be
written several letters in which were the words
JHESUS MARIA with a cross; and that it signified
that they to whom the letters were sent, were not
to obey their contents. In others, thou dost boast
that thou wilt kill all who do not obey thee; and

that when it comes to blows, it will be seen who has the better right from the King of heaven ; and of this thou dost say nothing was done, save by command and revelation of God.

To this the scholars say, thou art a pernicious, deceitful, cruel woman, thirsty for human blood, seditious, provoking to tyranny, and a blasphemer of God in attributing thy revelations to Him.

VII. Thou dost say, that by revelations which came to thee at seventeen years of age, thou didst leave thy parents' house against their will, at which they almost lost their senses; that thou didst go to Robert de Baudricourt, who, at thy request, gave thee a male habit and sword, and certain men to conduct thee to thy king ; and that when thou wast come to him, thou didst tell him thou wast sent to expel his adversaries; thou didst promise him a great dominion, and victory over his foes; and that God had sent thee to do it; and in all this thou dost say that thou didst act well, and in obedience to revelation from God.

To this the scholars answer, that thou art impious towards thy father and mother, disobedient to the command of honouring parents, scandalous, and a blasphemer of God; thou dost err in the faith, and thou hast made a rash and presumptuous promise.

VIII. Thou dost say, that of thyself thou didst spring from the tower of Beaurevoir, preferring rather to die than to be put into the hands of the

English, and to survive the destruction of Compiègne; that though St. Katherine and St. Margaret forbade thee, thou couldst not help it; and that though thou dost know it was a great sin to offend these saints, thou dost also know by thy *voices* that God forgave it thee, after thou hadst confessed it.

As to this the scholars say, it was pusillanimity verging on despair, and may be interpreted as a suicide. The assertion that this sin has been forgiven thee, is presumptuous and rash; and thou dost believe amiss in what concerns the free-will of man.

IX. Thou dost say that St. Katherine and St. Margaret have promised to conduct thee to paradise, if thou dost keep thy virginity which thou hast promised and vowed them; and of this thou art as certain as if thou wert in blessed glory already; and that thou dost not believe thou hast mortally sinned; for if thou wert in mortal sin, it seems to thee the saints would not visit thee every day as they do.

To this the scholars say, it is a rash and presumptuous assertion, a pernicious lie, a contradiction of the preceding article, and that thou dost think amiss in the Christian faith.

X. Thou dost say that God loves certain living persons more than thee, and that thou dost know it by revelations from St. Katherine and St. Margaret; that these saints speak French and not

English, because they are not of the English party;
and that since thou hast known that thy *voices*
were for the king, thou hast not loved the Burgundians.

As to this the scholars say, it is a presumptuous
assertion, a rash divination, a superstition, a blas-
phemy against St. Katherine and St. Margaret, and
a transgression of the principle of love to our neighbour.

XI. Thou dost say, with regard to the voices
and spirits which thou dost call St. Michael, St.
Katherine, and St. Margaret, that thou hast vener-
ated them, knelt to them, uncovered thy head,
kissed the ground where they had rested, and
vowed them thy virginity; that thou hast embraced
and invoked them; that thou hast obeyed their
counsel without asking the advice of thy curé or
any other priest; and nevertheless, thou dost believe these *voices* come on the part of God as firmly
as thou dost believe the Christian faith, and that
our Lord Jesus Christ has died. Thou dost say,
that if any evil spirit appeared to thee in the form
of St. Michael, thou shouldst discern it. Also
thou dost say, that of thy own will thou didst swear
not to tell the sign given to thy king; adding at
last, "Unless it were by God's command."

As to this the scholars say, supposing thou hast
had the apparitions and revelations of which thou
dost boast, in the manner in which thou dost assert,

that thou art an idolatress, an invocatress of devils;
that thou dost err in the faith, and affirm with temerity, and that thou hast made an unlawful oath.

XII. Thou dost say, that if the Church would have
thee do contrary to the commands thou dost assert
were given thee by God, thou wilt not for anything
obey; that thou knowest well what is in thy trial
came to thee by command of. God, and that it
would be impossible for thee to do contrary to it;
nor on it wilt thou refer thyself to the Church on
earth, nor to any living man, but to God only.
Thou dost say, this answer is not given of thy own
head, but by the command of God, though the
article of the faith, *Unam Sanctam Ecclesiam Catholicam*, has been many times declared to thee,
and though every Christian ought to submit all his
words and deeds to the Church militant, especially
in the case of revelations, and such things.

To this the scholars say, thou art schismatic,
thou dost think amiss of the unity and authority of
the Church; thou art an apostate, and thou dost
obstinately err in the faith.

Having thus run through the twelve fraudulent, wicked, calumnious articles, Pierre Morrice,
without pause, went on to deliver himself of his
monition, beginning,—"Now is the time, dearest
Jeanne, towards the end of your trial, to consider
what manner of words these are:" and concluding
with an exhortation, in the name of Christ's pas-

sion, to submit herself to the determination of the
Church, and to accept the correction of her judges.
" By doing this, you will save your soul, and redeem
your body from death; if you persevere in your
sin, be assured that you will incur the damnation
of your soul, and the destruction of your body.
From which, may Jesus Christ keep you."

The learned divine made an end, and Jeanne
was asked what she had to answer. For some
time she did not speak. The malicious travesty
of her words and deeds contained in the articles,
might well confound her, and Morrice's loving
effusion might well terrify her. For days she had
been haunted by a dreadful fear, a presentiment
that she should fail when the last push came; and
perhaps that very dread made her the more despe-
rately defiant now.

" If," said she, at length, " I were at judgment:
if I saw the fire kindled, and the faggots ablaze,
and the executioner ready to stir the fire : and if I
were in the fire, I would say no more, and to the
death I would maintain what I have said in the
trial ! "

The bishop immediately asked the promoter and
Jeanne if either had any more to say, and both
replying that they had not, he read a formula
declaring the CAUSE CONCLUDED, and assigned
the morrow for the prisoner to appear before her
judges to receive her sentence.

VII.

THE ABJURATION.

P to this point the Bishop of Beauvais's beautiful trial had prospered to his wishes marvellously. But its main object had yet to be compassed. When he opened the cause, he could hardly have anticipated the generous loyalty of his victim. If she died in it, without humbling herself to her judges, without in any way denying her inspiration, or contemning the king who had used her and abandoned her, the purpose of her adversaries would be but half served. Perhaps less than half served; perhaps utterly defeated. The popular mind has a tendency to embrace beliefs maintained to the death; and if Jeanne could so maintain the verity of her revelations, some of which none could deny had been gloriously fulfilled, dead, she would have a following such as in her day of honour she had never numbered. What, therefore, had to be accom-

plished now was to bring her to make a public
abjuration which should degrade her, and Charles
by means of her, which should give her judges the
opportunity of displaying the merciful disposition
befitting their ecclesiastical character, and leave it
still in the power of those who desired it, to bring
her to that relapse which the Inquisition never
pardoned, and which would consign her to the fire
inevitably at last.

This crowning success depended entirely upon
Jeanne. If she persevered with constant fortitude,
then she would be handed over to the secular
power, condemned, and burnt at once, and repent-
ant France might weep for her as the truest, most
noble of women. If she yielded, she would be lost
in the esteem of the people, clothed with shame
and self-contempt, and she would have a respite,
long or short in proportion to her own powers of
endurance, and the patience of the bishop and his
accomplices; but her death was as sure in the one
case as the other.

She was not left much to her own thoughts that
day. After Pierre Morrice had acquitted himself
of his admonition before the judges and select
assessors, he obtained leave to reason with her in
private; so did Châtillon, whom Thomas de Courcelles accompanied to her prison. The Bishop of
Noyon went, Martin l'Advenu went, and Loiselleur hardly ever left her. Jeanne listened and

learned, and still with that forewarning of ultimate failure creeping coldly over her will, held on to her original idea that God ought first to be served, and grasped with a more vivid realisation her secondary idea, that to submit to the Church would be to allow that she had done ill; to consent, in fact, to those XII. Articles, and the opinions of the scholars upon them, that she had heard in the morning.

The miseries of captivity had taken hold upon her, but her mind and conscience were as lucid in view of her peril as they had ever been. From the various instructions of her faithful or deceitful counsellors, she had thought out a clear view of every means left of evading it ; and struggling with her fatal presentiment of weakness, resolved yet to fight a good fight for her life and her truth. And she was likely to be hard beset, and tried with sore temptations. What was the past tenor of Loiselleur's advice to her can only be conjectured; but on this occasion, Manchon, the notary, heard him pleading with her energetically.

" Jeanne, believe me, you may be saved if you will. Accept your woman's dress, and do whatever you are bidden, or you are in certain danger of death. And if you do what I tell you, you will be saved ; no harm will befal you ; you will find yourself very well off, and you will be restored to the Church; your chains will be removed, and you will be released from the English."

She had this seductive promise to think of all
night, and early in the morning Jean Beaupère
visited her with a word of exhortation. "Jeanne,"
said the dry doctor, who thought her so subtle but
not corrupt, "you will soon be taken out to the
grave-yard of the Abbey of Saint-Ouen, to be
preached to before the people. Now, if you are a
good Christian, you will say there, on the scaffold,
that all your words and deeds you will submit to
the ordinances of holy mother Church, and especially of your ecclesiastical judges." She gave him
to understand that she had in her mind some ex-
pedient of submission ; and he left her.

This public sermon, which would be followed
either by Jeanne's recantation or execution, was
to be preached by Guillaume Erard. When the
bishop delegated to him the onerous duty, he
wished himself in Flanders, and said the task was
most repugnant to him. And well it might be.
He was on terms of friendship with Gerard Machet,
confessor of Charles VII.; and Gerard Machet had
.held the Maid to be the envoy of God. But the
bishop knew the man of his choice. Erard had
the temper and spirit of a born advocate, and
whatever cause he undertook to plead for, he put
his heart into it, and letting honour and conscience go, urged it with his utmost eloquence.

A striking scene had been arranged for the
solemn ceremonial of which the close might be so

tragical, and the Church was represented in it by a crowd of dignified ecclesiastics. In the centre of the vast grave-yard of the beautiful Abbey of Saint-Ouen had been erected two scaffolds, facing each other. On one appeared the two judges, the Cardinal of England, the Bishops of Norwich, Noyon, and Thourenne, the Abbots of Feçamp, Saint-Ouen, Cormeilles, Jumièges, Bec-Helluin, Mont-Saint-Michel, and Mortemar, the Prior of Longueville, some thirty of the assessors, and several distinguished strangers and members of the English court. On the second scaffold was Guillaume Erard, the preacher, and near him Jeanne d'Arc, put forward in full view of the people, and confronting them and her judges with an air of self-possession, and, as it seemed to some, of gay mockery, as if she fancied they were only met together to enact a comedy. Close by her stood Massieu and Mauger Parmentier. Loiselleur and Martin l'Advenu were also there,—Loiselleur ready at her ear to whisper evil counsel; and the notaries, Manchon and Boisguillaume. The whole graveyard was a silent crowd, and in the space between the scaffolds, if Jeanne regarded the curious witnesses wondering at her, she must have seen Haimond de Macy, and Jean Moreau, a man from her own country; Taquel, Monnet, and the inquisitive citizens of Rouen who had intruded into her prison at her first coming.

Erard took for his text the words of St. John—
"A branch cannot bear fruit, except it abide in the
vine." He then began his sermon by proving the
necessity of submission to the Church; and for the
publication of Jeanne's iniquities, and the salutary
warning and edification of the people, many of
whom thought she was being sacrificed to please
the English, he recited the XII. Articles, and the
condemnation the doctors had pronounced against
them and herself.

"Behold the pride of this woman!" cried he, and
warming to his theme as he went on, he addressed
her in the coarsest terms of reprobation. Presently,
exalting his voice higher, he began to shriek plain-
tively:—"O noble house of France! who until now
hast kept thyself from monstrous things, and hast
been ever the protectress of the faith, hast thou
been so deceived as to trust in a heretic and schismatic? Great is the pity! Ah! France, thou hast
been much deceived; thou hast been always the
most Christian land, and Charles, who calls himself
thy king and governor, has trusted like a heretic
and schismatic, such as he is, to the words and deeds
of a useless, defamed woman, full of all dishonour;
and not he only, but all the clergy in his obedience
and lordship, by whom she was examined, and not
rebuked. It is to *thee* I speak, Jeanne," raising his
hand, and pointing at her with the finger, "and I
tell thee that thy king is a heretic and schismatic!"

Jeanne took this as a challenge to speak herself, and spoke up boldly for Charles, to screen him from blame. " Say of me what you like, but let the king be : he is a good Christian, and he did *not* trust in me ;" and as the preacher held on still in the same strain of abuse, she interrupted him again, exclaiming—" Saving your reverence, sir, that is not true ! I dare say and swear to you, on pain of my life, that the king is the noblest Christian of all Christians, and who the best loves the faith and the Church ; and he is not such as you say !"

" Make her hold her peace !" cried Erard and the Bishop of Beauvais together to Massieu.

Soon after, the preacher brought his too zealous sermon to an end ; but his attack on Charles had roused all Jeanne's spirit, and when he began to admonish her to submit to the Church, she had good courage to withstand him.

" Here," said he, " are my lords the judges, who have again and again summoned and required you to submit all your words and deeds to our holy mother Church; for in your words and deeds there are many things which, as it seems to the scholars, are neither good to say nor to maintain."

" I will answer you," replied Jeanne, distinctly. " As for submission to the Church, I have told them to let all the works I have done, and my words be sent to Rome, to our holy father the Pope, to whom, and to God *first*, I refer myself.

For as to the things I have said and done, I have
done them on the part of God."

In furtherance of her adversaries' greedy anxiety
to elicit from Jeanne some excuse or plea for herself, which might redound to the dishonour of the
king, Erard suggested to her what one of the
consultants on the XII. Articles had given as his
opinion—namely, that Charles and his ministers
had trained her only to serve their political purposes. But her loyal soul recoiled from the base
temptation, and she answered him with disappoint-
ing plainness.

"Of my words and deeds I charge *no* man—
neither my king nor any other! If there be any
fault in them, it is mine, and mine only."

"Then will you revoke your words and deeds
which are reproved?" demanded the preacher.

"I refer myself upon them to God, and to our
holy father the Pope."

"That is not enough. We cannot send so far
as Rome to bring the Pope here. Every Ordinary
is judge in his own diocese ; therefore it is necessary that you submit to our holy mother Church,
and to what the scholars and ecclesiastics, learned
in such matters, have said and determined about
you and your works."

Jeanne's will and conscience did battle still with
her fears and failing heart. She clung to her first
declaration, and thrice in vain was she admonished

in set terms to submit. Then Erard tried another manœuvre. Two formulas of abjuration had been prepared—one very strongly worded and elaborated for her to sign, composed by the bishop's chaplain ; the other about the length of a *pater noster*, less likely to drive her to despairing resistance, which contained the heads only, for her to repeat before the people if she recanted. This short document Erard handed to Massieu, bidding him read it to her, and telling her significantly: " Jeanne, thou wilt abjure and sign that schedule."

" I do not know what it is to abjure," replied she.

Massieu was ordered to explain it to her. The good priest would fain have excused himself. He saw she was either unconscious or incredulous of her peril. Loiselleur had always entertained her with the hope of life ; but Erard reiterated his command, and then he tried to make her seriously grasp the one point it was essential she should understand. " To abjure means, Jeanne, that if you ever go contrary to any of the points written in this schedule, you will be burnt." Then taking courage to help her, he added : " And, therefore, I advise you to appeal to the Church Universal, whether you ought to abjure them or not."

Jeanne could trust Massieu. She looked at Erard, and said firmly, " I appeal to the Church Universal whether I ought to abjure them or not."

"Thou shalt abjure them at once, or thou shalt be burnt!" hissed the preacher, vehemently.

Loiselleur assailed her on the other side tenderly : "Jeanne, you *must* yield, and consent to wear a woman's dress."

"I put on this and wear it, because it is more fit and prudent to appear as a man amongst men-at-arms," said she, addressing Erard.

They continued to urge her, mixing menaces and prayers, until she grew thoroughly exasperated, and exclaimed, "All that I have done, all that I do, is well done, and I have done well to do it!"

It seemed as if she would vanquish her adversaries, and die bravely as she had lived. There was nothing left for them but to have recourse to their last terrors. She had been brought to Saint-Ouen in a sort of carriage drawn by four horses, and the executioner was shown to her, waiting by it to carry her away to burn her. Two sentences had been prepared—one of condemnation, the other to be given in case she abjured. The bishop set himself to read the first, casting her off from the Church, very slowly, the sonorous rumble of its awful phrases forming a chorus to the low, urgent pleadings and urgings of the priests, which never ceased. Erard could not bear to be defeated ; he had no scruples how he won, so that he conquered Jeanne's will at last. Threats had failed, and he tried bribes and promises. She must make haste to repent: if she let the judge come to his last word, she was lost. He gave her no moment of pause to cry to God that He would strengthen her weakness.

"Jeanne, we pity thee so much! Thou *must* revoke what thou hast said, or we must abandon thee to the secular power."

She defended herself still. "I have done nothing amiss. I believe the twelve articles of the faith, and the ten commandments; and I will refer what I have done and said to Rome."

The bishop was half way through the sentence. Erard tried his last trick. "Thou *must* abjure, Jeanne. If thou wilt do what thou art counselled to do, thou shalt be delivered out of prison."

"You try very hard to seduce me!" she exclaimed, bitterly.

"O Jeanne, why will you die?" chimed in another voice, and, at the same moment, in the crowd rose angry cries, mutterings of men who see they are going to be disappointed of their prey. The horror of that cruel sound, and the prayers of the priests prevailed; and Jeanne's good angel let her for the moment go.

"*I will submit!*"

The bishop instantly stopt—he had been very near the end.

"My lord of Beauvais favours the woman," grumbled an English priest, the chaplain of the cardinal.

"There is no favouring in such a case!" angrily retorted the judge. "It is the duty of my profession to watch for the salvation of her body and soul. You have insulted me, and I will not pass it over without reparation."

The chaplain was not disposed to recall his words, and the cardinal interposed to end the scene, begging them to say no more, and especially telling his own man to hold his tongue. The able bishop had taken very few persons into his confidence, and nothing could have been more salutary for his reputation than this public, unexpected charge from the blundering, dull Englishman that he favoured the poor victim he was wilily hunting to death.

Jeanne had now to recite, and to sign the act of her abjuration. She said she could not read, and Massieu pronounced each phrase, and she repeated it after him. Haimond de Macy, who was in the crowd close by, and could see and hear everything she did, observed that she was smiling derisively as she went through the formula, and several others near said she was making a jest of it, and it was no abjuration. It ran to this effect :—

"I Jeanne, called *the Maid*, miserable sinner, since I have learnt the coil of error in which I was

held, and by God's grace am returned to our holy
mother Church, confess that I have grievously
sinned, in lyingly feigning to have had revelations
and apparitions from God, by the angels, and St.
Margaret and St. Katherine; in wearing a dissolute
dress, against the decency of nature, and armour,
and my hair cut round like a man. In many ways
I have erred in the faith, which, by the grace of
God and the good counsel of the doctors, with free
heart and will I now abjure, in everything submitting myself to the correction of our holy mother
Church and your good justice."

As soon as Jeanne had spoken this recantation,
the longer schedule was laid before her to sign.
Whether she did not understand why it was sub-
stituted for the one she had just pronounced, or
whether she suspected some deceit, does not appear,
but she said: "Let this schedule be seen by the
clergy and the Church, in whose hands I ought
to be put; and if they counsel me to sign it, and
to do the things I am bidden to do, I will obey
them."

" Sign *now*, otherwise thou shalt end thy life in
the fire to-day !" yelled Erard.

" Better sign than burn !" murmured Jeanne.
Taking a pen Massieu offered her, she laughed and
made a round O at the foot of the document, saying: " I cannot write."

Laurence Callot, one of the English secretaries,

who was on the scaffold, seized her hand, and guided it to sign her name, JEHANNE. She then made a cross by the scrawl, and the act of abjuration being completed, the Bishop of Beauvais asked the Cardinal of England what he was to do.

" Mitigate the sentence," was the answer, and the judge proceeded to mitigate it accordingly.

The document tediously began with a recitation of the duty of Christian pastors, which was followed by an enumeration of Jeanne's great crimes, and was concluded thus—" As, after being long charitably warned and waited for, you come back at last, by the grace of God, with a contrite heart and a faith unfeigned, as we believe; as you have revoked your errors aloud, and publicly abjured your heresy, in obedience to ecclesiastical ordinance, we release you from the excommunication you have incurred, if you return with a true and sincere heart, and if you observe the things that we shall prescribe. But, since you have sinned against God and the Church, we condemn you, in our grace and moderation, to pass the rest of your days in prison, on the bread of sorrow and the water of anguish, there to weep and lament your sins, and commit no more for the future."

Jeanne stood and heard it all, and felt how she had been entrapped by false promises, until Loiselleur came up to her congratulatory and grinning:

" Jeanne, you have done a good day's work, and please God, have saved your soul ! "

She turned from him abruptly, and addressing her judges with loud indignation, said : " Now, you men of the Church, you have condemned me, take me, some of you, into the Church prisons; do not leave me any longer in the hands of these English!"

The English had gone so far in expressing their dissatisfaction at not having her to burn at once, as to throw stones at the clergy on the scaffold, and to shout that they had earned the king's money ill. Her demand was of such palpable propriety and justice, that several ecclesiastics, the Prior of Longueville particularly, required the Bishop of Beauvais to accede to it. But this transference of her to the episcopal prison might have defeated the notable conclusion he had yet to put to his beautiful trial; and without condescending to give either reason or reply to those who spoke for the hapless prisoner, he coolly said to the guards who had her in charge: " Carry her back to the place you brought her from." And she was carried back to the castle.

In the afternoon, Jeanne was visited in her prison by the vice-inquisitor, who came accompanied by Loiselleur, Midy, Thomas de Courcelles, Pierre Morrice, Brother Isambard de la Pierre, and a few others. Loiselleur and Morrice appeared, bringing her female clothing.

The inquisitor, who had been little more than a lay-figure on her trial, as regarded his duty, was apparently anxious that she should be saved; for after representing to her what mercy God had shown her, and what tenderness and indulgence she had experienced from the ecclesiastics who had received her into the Church again, he exhorted her to take heed of returning to her former ways; warning her that if she did, her penitence would be no more accepted, but she would be totally relinquished by the Church.

Her wild defiant mood of the morning was past. She was altogether humble and subdued. She said she would be obedient. The inquisitor then told her that she must accept her woman's dress; for so the Church commanded. And for a fore-taste of its tender mercies, and of her own deep humiliation, she was bidden to unclothe herself in the presence of the council, and put it on.

When it was done, she lifted her tearful, ashamed, entreating face: " Would they not take her into their prison."

No. The inquisitor slunk off, the miserable coward, and the rest followed him; Brother Isambard the only man amongst them with a spark of pity for her. And so she was left to sup her sorrow to the dregs.

VIII.

THE RELAPSE. '

THE English soldiers were grievously disappointed by the Maid's abjuration. They never expected to prosper in arms, while she was alive to pray against them with her mysterious *counsel*, as she had prayed when they were besieging Compiègne with Burgundy. Lord Suffolk and Lord Arundel had gone with an army to the attack of Louviers which La Hire held, but none of their men thought they should take it, until they had got the Witch of the Armagnacs burned. The citizens of Rouen, many of whom heartily rejoiced in her escape, made merry over the fears of their foreign masters. Very real these fears were, but their courage and patience were not to be long tried. When the Bishop of Beauvais seemed to let Jeanne go, he knew very well where and how she might be caught again.

Nearly all the great monks but the Abbot of
Feçamp, who had vigorously supported the bishop
from the beginning of the cause, now quitted Rouen
and retired to their houses, thankful, no doubt, that
the momentous affair had not ended in a barbarous
execution. It was rather singular that the four
leading Paris counsellors did not also, now that
their work was done, imitate their flight, and make
haste back to the University with the news. But
perhaps the University would have given them only
a churlish welcome, since their judgment had fallen
so far short of the notable and great reparation she
had piously recommended to the king, as essential
to the public good and the Divine honour. At all
events, Beaupère, Midy, Morrice, and De Courcelles
stayed on at Rouen. Feuillet, who had heard all
the examinations of Jeanne, both public and private, had left after the monition given to her, sick
in prison ; and Texier had remained behind in
Paris, when he went thither with Beaupère and
Midy, bearing the XII. Articles. It is possible
these two doctors declined to accompany their more
zealous brethren to the end of the bishop's beautiful trial, foreseeing what that end was to be.

A bad deed set well a-going has a natural tendency to accomplish itself. In sending Jeanne
back to the castle after her abjuration, the bishop
was sure of a perfect success. But he was very
close about it. Even the Earl of Warwick thought

the matter concluded ; for he quitted Saint-Ouen
growling that the king's affairs went badly, and the
woman would not be burnt. The English council
had been at an enormous charge to purchase her,
at another enormous charge to hire judges and
divines to prove her the devil-inspired being such
an incubus on their prosperity must certainly be ;
and after all this cost and pains, she was left alive
on their hands : terrifying the imaginations of their
soldiers a hundred miles off, cooling their valour as
effectually as when she met them in the field.

One of the assessors hearing the English rage
to this tune, bade them significantly not fret themselves. " We shall know how to take her again !
you shall be satisfied anon." The length of the
trial had been a sore drag on the impatience of her
adversaries ; and amongst other excuses put forward for its delays, was one, that the Maid had
pleaded in bar of judgment that she was with child :
—an infamous calumny which was the popular belief in England for generations.

Five or six *houspilleurs*, the scum of the army,
were considered now the fittest keepers for the
dreaded witch, and she had been given to them. On
the very morrow of her abjuration, a rumour ran
through the city that she did not in anywise repent,
but was returning to all her errors. The bishop
was apprized of it. He professed neither astonishment nor regret, but satanically formal and decent

in acting out his part, he sent Jean Beaupère and Nicole Midy to exhort her to persevere in her promises, lest she should incur the peril of relapse. They set off to the castle, but the key of her prison was not forthcoming, and they could not get admittance to see her. While they waited about, a few noisy English soldiers came blustering and threatening them, and the brave doctors manfully ran away.

God knows the secrets of the two dreadful days between Jeanne's abjuration and her relapse. If she was the monster of pride her judges declared, they put her in the way of having her pride pulled down. Her sufferings broke her spirit, and broke her heart. She cast herself helplessly again on her old *counsel*, and she was saved from the last dishonour, and its despair. But repentance seized upon her with a thousand pangs. Messages of rebuke and condemnation for what she had done, thrilled in her conscience and in her ears; but it was still her familiar divine *voices* that brought them, not taunting fiends. And even with rebuke they gave her comfort, telling her there was pity for her in heaven because she had fallen.

She endured the cruel indignities of her vile keepers, and of others who entered her prison to exult in her calamity, as part of the penance to which her pious judges had condemned her. But she could not endure them long. On the third morning after the scene at Saint-Ouen, Trinity Sunday it was, she woke up to the sound of the church bells, and asked her guards to unchain her, and let her rise. One of them unlocked her fetters, took away her female clothing, and threw over her her old dress, which had been put into a bag, and left in her room. The others stood by. Jeanne looked at them with pleading anguish, and entreated them to let her have the things her judges had commanded her to wear.

"Sirs," she said, "you know this is forbidden me. Without erring I cannot put it on."

They mocked her tears, and thrust her woman's dress into the bag. She knelt to them, she prayed to them. For an hour, for two hours, till noon, she was at their feet. When she wearied them, they struck her. One, more daring or more wicked than the rest, offered her even grosser violence, and she resenting it, he loaded her with blows. The *good justice* of the Church had put her obedience to too severe a proof. Better death, though she reached it by the cruel path of the flames, than the tyranny of these evil men! When they left her, she looked at the forbidden garments, and at last, to cover herself, she put them on. And when it was done, she felt better at ease.

By and by, came in witnesses, and cried, "Behold the Witch relapsed!"

Lord Warwick came, saw, and was satisfied.

Messengers were sent to bring the bishop, the inquisitor, the promoter, the doctors, the masters, the
notaries—all left in Rouen who had been engaged
on her trial, to certify her relapse.

The bishop was not at home, but many of his
assistants came at once, openly expressing their
regret at the cause for which they were summoned.
Pierre Morrice especially seemed grieved : and
Marguerie was suspicious. There were a number
of soldiers in the castle-yard strongly inclined to
fall foul of the ecclesiastics, who were, they said, all
false traitors together. Marguerie began to answer
defiantly that it was not enough to know the
prisoner had put on her man's dress—he should
like to know *why* she had put it on. The soldiers
grew furious, and no longer confining themselves
to words and curses, they drove the whole pack
of priests out of the castle-yard, and over the
bridge, with so much tumult and violence, that
Manchon, the notary, when sent for again, refused
to go without a safe-conduct from Lord Warwick.
The consequence was, that none of the assessors
saw Jeanne that day ; but witnesses more than
enough had seen her. In the evening her woman's
clothing was restored to her, but she did not avail
herself of it. She had repented of her sin against
God and her conscience, and was ready to redeem it, if needs must be, by the sacrifice of her
life.

The next morning, the judges and the promoter
went to the prison, to investigate the state and disposition of Jeanne. There had arrived before them
Venderez, De Courcelles, Hayton, Brother Isambard de la Pierre, and three ecclesiastics who had
taken no part in the trial, Jacques le Camus, Nicolas
Bertin, and Julian Flosquet. John Grey was also
present, and Manchon, the notary.

Jeanne was dressed in the habit so often denounced by her judges, but she was greatly changed
in herself. Brother Isambard, for pity and compassion, could hardly bear to look at her. Her
countenance was full of tears; in her eyes there
was the anguish of an endurance overwrought and
broken down. She had been a long while at bay,
and now she was taken. The hunters had proved
themselves more subtle than their quarry, and
through the simulated trouble of the bishop's manner, there pierced a triumph that he could not conceal. He began by asking her why she had put on
again that shameless dress which, in obedience to
the Church, she had laid by. Jeanne had poured
out her sorrows to Massieu often, and to Brother
Isambard she had complained that her keepers
used her with barbarous indignity; but she had
never brought herself to speak openly of her humi-
liations before the dignified, sanctified bishop and
his great colleagues. Nor did she now. She gave
her questioner several evasive replies; said she had

put on the dress of herself, and that she never understood she had made oath not to take it again. He asked her for what cause she had put it on.

" It is more lawful for me to wear the dress of a man, being amongst men, than the dress of a woman," replied she. The bishop reminded her of her promise. She answered that the churchmen had not kept *their* promise to her : namely, that she should go to mass, and receive her Saviour, and have her irons taken off. Once more he urged her to remember how she had abjured. To this she said, piteously :—" I would rather *die* than live in chains ! But if you will take me out of them, and let me go to mass, and put me into a quiet prison, and give me a woman to keep me, I *will* be good —I will do what the Church bids me !"

Her adversary made her no answer, but immediately went on to discover in what other points of her recantation she had failed. He inquired if, since Thursday, she had heard her *voices.* She said she had,—dissimulating nothing of the fatal truth.

" And what have they told you, Jeanne ?"

" That God had sent me word by St. Katherine and St. Margaret how great was the pity that I had consented to the treason of abjuring to save my life ; and that I damned myself to save my life."

" Did your *voices* tell you before Thursday what
you would do on that day ?"

" Yes. And on the scaffold they bade me answer
the preacher boldly. I call that preacher a false
preacher ; for he said many things of me that I
never did !"

" Do you still maintain that you were sent to
your king on the part of God?"

" If I were to say that God did not send me, I
should condemn myself ; for true it is that God did
send me."

" Do you still believe that your *voices* are St.
Katherine and St. Margaret ?"

" Yes ; and from God."

" Have they reproached you for your abjuration ?"

" They have told me it was a great wickedness
to confess that I had not well done. For fear of
the fire I said what I said !"

The bishop knew that. He asked her about the
crown—the sign given to the king.

" Upon my trial, I told you the truth of all as
well as I knew how," replied Jeanne.

" On the scaffold at Saint-Ouen did you not confess that it was lyingly you had boasted your *voices*
were St. Katherine and St. Margaret ?"

" I did not understand that I was saying or doing
so. I never meant to deny that my apparitions
were St. Katherine and St. Margaret. Whatever

I did was for fear of the fire! But *now*, I would rather make my penance once for all and *die*, than suffer any longer what I suffer in this prison!"

In answer to some further interrogatories of the bishop, she said—"I have done nothing against God or the faith, whatever you may have made me revoke; and as for what was in the schedule of abjuration, I did not understand it. If you, my judges, will put me into a safe place, I will take again my woman's dress; but of the rest I will do nothing."

This heard, the bishop, the inquisitor, and the counsellors left her: without answer, and without further notice than she had received before, of her approaching fate, of which she always had been,— of which she was perhaps yet, at heart, incredulous.

On the following morning took place the-final consultation of the assessors on the Maid's trial. The judges convoked them to meet at a certain hour in the archiepiscopal chapel, and they assembled to the number of twenty-nine. There appeared six ecclesiastics besides, who had not given sentence at the first judgment; and the three physicians, Tiphaine, De la Chambre, and Desjardins. Fifteen, who had concurred in the first judgment, absented themselves from the second. Amongst the most distinguished of the seceders were Jean Beaupère, who had quitted Rouen, on his way to

Bâle, the morning Jeanne's relapse was certified; Raoul Roussel, chancellor and treasurer of Rouen cathedral, Raoul Sauvage, Pierre Minier, and the Abbot of Cormeille. There were, however, more than enough to go through the formalities of the occasion. The terrible machinery of the Inquisition, which the bishop had pressed into his service, moved from the point of a relapse inevitably deathwards, and those who came together had no choice but to let it go on.

The bishop gave a brief narration of how Jeanne had been admonished of her errors by Pierre Morrice,¶ in the presence of the Bishops of Thourenne and Noyon, and others, and had been instructed in the opinion of the University upon them. She had still persisted in her damnable propositions, he said, and the cause had therefore been concluded, and a day assigned her to hear her sentence in form of law. He then detailed how, after the sermon at Saint-Ouen, she had continued obstinate until the sentence was nearly read, when she said she would submit, and according to a schedule which was read to her, she did revoke and abjure her errors, signing the schedule with her own hand. And the same day she was absolved, and her punishment enjoined; and she accepted her woman's dress. But the night following and since, deluded by the devil, she said her *voices* and spirits had come to her, and told her many things.

And finally, she had rejected her woman's dress, and resumed the other; on hearing of which, he and the inquisitor had gone to the prison with certain assistants, had seen her, and interrogated her. He then ordered Manchon's minute of the examination to be read before the assessors; and this done, they were called upon to give their sentences.

Nicolas Venderez began. "She is a heretic; let her be abandoned to secular justice, praying it to spare her death and mutilation of members." This last clause was quite fallacious: it sounded merciful in the mouths of ecclesiastics, but it was perfectly understood that when the Church cut off a heretic from its communion, the secular power must, without delay, consign the victim to the fire.

The Abbot of Feçamp followed. "She is relapsed. Nevertheless it is good the schedule of her abjuration should be again read to her, and the word of God on it expounded. And this done, let our judges declare her a heretic, and abandon her to secular justice, praying it to spare her death and mutilation of members."

Jean Pinchon came next—a licentiate of canon-law. "The woman is relapsed: the further mode of proceeding, I refer to the doctors of divinity." Pinchon had no imitators.

The majority of the assessors, amongst whom were Erard, Châtillon, Hayton, Fabri, Morrice, Loiselleur, De Courcelles, and Brother Isambard, adopted

the advice of the Abbot of Feçamp. Fabri, who
began by thinking Jeanne inspired, added to his
sentence that she was "obstinate, contumacious,
and disobedient." Thomas de Courcelles and
Brother Isambard agreed in adding to theirs:
"Let her be warned that there is now no hope
of her temporal life, and let her be still tenderly
admonished for the salvation of her soul."

When each of the assessors had pronounced his
verdict, the judges thanked them, and said they
should proceed forward against Jeanne, as relapsed,
according to law and reason. A citation was drawn
up in their names, calling on her to appear before
them the next morning at eight o'clock, in the Old
Market of Rouen, there to hear and undergo her
sentence. This citation was delivered to Massieu
to execute, with orders not to carry it to the
condemned prisoner until the hour arrived.

When the council broke up and dispersed, the
Earl of Warwick was waiting in the court of the
palace with some other English, impatient to hear
the result of their deliberations. As the bishop
came out of the chapel, Warwick hurried to meet
him, and Brother Isambard and Brother Martin
l'Advenu following close behind the judge, heard
him say in a voice of lively satisfaction, waving his
hand to the others, as he walked away with the
earl: "Farewell, farewell! Be of good cheer: it
is done!"

IX.

THE MARTYRDOM.

FOR the execution of the heroic Maid who had turned for ever the tide of their prosperity in France, the English authorities made solemn and imposing preparations. Near the church of Saint-Saviour, in the Old Market, then a vast open space, they raised a lofty mound of rubbish, on which was piled the wood to burn her. The stake reared itself from the midst of the faggots, high and dreadful, that, bound upon it, she might make her *notable and great reparation*, visible to the eyes of all the people.

Two scaffolds were set up opposite, at some distance : one to receive the judges, the secular magistrates, Nicole Midy, who was to preach the death-sermon, and the Maid, until sentence had been pronounced ; the other, for the accommodation of the Cardinal-bishop of Winchester, and any other prelates and personages who might feel it a duty or a pleasure to assist at the tragedy.

The Bishop of Beauvais had commissioned Brother Martin l'Advenu to announce her fate to Jeanne, and to prepare her for it; and at an early hour of the morning, accompanied by another Dominican, Jean Tout-mouillé, he made his way to the castle. Admitted into her prison, he told her wherefore he was come, by what death she was to die, and when:—She believed it at last, and let go all hope.

"Alas!" cried she, casting up her hands in a passion of grief and dread; "alas! how can they treat me so horribly and cruelly, that my whole body, pure and undefiled, must be to-day consumed, and turned to ashes? Oh, I would rather be beheaded seven times than burnt! Alas! if I had been in the prison of the Church, to which I submitted, and guarded by its servants, instead of by my enemies and adversaries, it would not so miserably have befallen me as this. Oh, I appeal to God, the Great Judge, against the wrongs and dishonours that they do me!"

The words of the monk, exhorting her with patience and penitence to suffer all, fell on deafened ears. It was not death she shrank from, but *this* death, this death of exquisite torture, and uttermost shame. Her body that she had kept as the very temple of the Holy Spirit, was not deemed worthy of the soft repose of earth! was to be blasted in the cruel fire, dispersed in air; its ashes to be cast abroad on the highway, and trodden under foot of men; or cast into the deep river, and borne down to the sea. The vision of her near and dreadful end pressed darkly upon her, and for a little while shut out all view of heaven.

Brother Martin bided his time, and when her passion had wailed itself into sobbing silence, he spoke comfort to her. Then presently the black cloud of mortal fears began to break, and drift away; and there returned upon her that strong assurance of salvation that had upheld her through her long martyrdom.

Pierre Morrice came in, to whom she said: "Master Pierre, where shall I be to-day at evening?"

"Hast thou not a good hope in God, Jeanne?" he asked her.

"I have, and, Christ helping me, I shall be in Paradise!"

Loiselleur entered next, haggard and eager. Only the wretch himself knew fully how he had deceived and betrayed Jeanne; but it was whispered about in Rouen that he had disguised himself like a St. Katherine, and going to her prison in the dusk hours, had taught her to defy her judges, to refuse submission to the Church obstinately, and to maintain that confident air which had prejudiced against her such men as Fabri. Much of this was probably idle talk : but he had certainly encouraged her natural hope of life, and ultimate deliverance. How he had encouraged it was between himself and his accomplices ; but a very guilty conscience towards her he had, and by and by, he betrayed it. He fought off its pangs yet awhile, and in his disturbance, tried to extort from her something to salve them. The more criminal she, the less his guilt, the less wicked his treason.

" Jeanne!" cried he, "there is nothing to think of *now* but the salvation of your soul. Tell us all the truth about your revelations. Did any angel bring your king a crown, as you said on your trial ?"

She confessed to her fiction, but had strength still to keep Charles's secret. She said that by the angel she meant herself, as sent from God; and by the sign of the crown, a pledge that the king should recover all the kingdom of France.

" And of the angels that you said accompanied you ?" inquired Morrice.

" They were indeed there, a very great multitude," she replied.

" And these apparitions were *real*, Jeanne ? If they were, they must have been evil spirits," urged Morrice.

" They were real, indeed ! I saw them with my eyes, and heard them with my ears. Be they good spirits or be they evil spirits, they did appear to me!"

"Tell us plainly *how* they appeared to you."

Words ill served her to express the hallucinations of her ecstatic moments; but, as well as they could gather from her broken sentences, she said that they appeared like a vast cloud of shadowy faces; and the *voices* she heard best when the bells rang for complines and matins.

"Many persons, Jeanne, believe they hear words in the bells," said Morrice.

Here the bishop came in with the vice-inquisitor, Venderez, De Courcelles, and Jacques le Camus. When Jeanne, through her tear-clouded eyes, saw her adversary, she cried out, "Bishop, I die by you!"

He began to remonstrate with her in his dulcet way. "Ah! Jeanne, take it patiently. You die because you have not kept the promise you made us, and because you have returned to your first iniquities."

"Alas! alas!" she went on, weeping again, yet indignant, "if you had put me into the prison of the Church, and given me fit and proper keepers, this had not happened. Therefore, I appeal to God against you!"

"Come, Jeanne!" retorted the wicked judge, unable to deny her charge, but seeking his excuse; "you always told us that your *voices* promised you should be *delivered*. You see now how they have deceived you; tell us the truth."

" I see well that I was deceived !"

" Then, if you see you were deceived, do you believe it was by good spirits, or by evil spirits?"

" I do not know ! I leave it to you churchmen !"

For a brief moment, her faith in the inspiration of her life seemed to waver, and all about her was dark again. The judges retired, leaving her with Brother Martin, that she might make her last confession. He aided her very carefully and tenderly, and when it was done, he gave her absolution in the penitential form; and she most humbly and earnestly entreating that she might have her Saviour before she died, he sent Massieu to ask the bishop if he might administer the viaticum to her.

When Massieu entered the room to which the judges had withdrawn, and delivered the message, the bishop consulted a minute with those present, and then said, abruptly, " Yes, let him give her the viaticum, and whatever else she asks for."

Massieu hastened back with this permission, and Pierre Morrice went to the chapel and brought the Eucharist from the altar, but without taper or stole for the priest. Brother Martin, displeased at the negligence and irreverence, sent Massieu to fetch a light; and while a procession of monks, bearing torches and chanting a litany, *Pray for her*, were bringing the host, with solemn pomp, through the thronged streets, it was being quietly administered to her in the presence of only a few priests.

Jeanne knelt, weeping great tears ; and holding the consecrated wafer in his hands before her, Brother Martin said, "Do you believe that this is the body of Jesus Christ?"

She answered, with a burst of such contrition and anguish as no words could utter, " I *do* believe, and that *He* alone can set me free !"

The time was now come. The Maid was unclothed, and arrayed in the mourning robe in which the Inquisition always sent its penitents to the fire; while on her head was bound a grotesque thing, shaped like a mitre, and inscribed in large characters with the words, *Heretique, Relapse, Apostate, Idolatre.* She was then taken down to the castleyard, where waited a carriage with four horses to convey her to the place of execution. A guard of five or six hundred soldiers was ready to escort it, all armed, their swords and lances glittering in the bright May morning sun. They were very glad. Let her remember Orleans, remember Jargeau, remember Patay ! They had waited long for their revenge, but it was sure at last. The Witch wept like the veriest woman ; but tears could not quench fire ; and soon she would palsy their arms, and put swiftness into their feet no more !

Martin l'Advenu and Massieu mounted into the carriage with her, and it was about to move, when the miserable Loiselleur, seized with a rending remorse, broke his way through the guards, and climbing up, flung himself at her feet, crying, "Pardon, Jeanne, pardon!" Whether she saw him in her tears, or understood him, could not be known; for the soldiers dragged him away, and cast him behind them; and the Earl of Warwick, who was standing by, warned him that if he meant to save his life, he had better make haste, and get out of Rouen.

It was nearly nine o'clock when the dreadful procession took its way towards the Old Market. Nicolas de Houppeville, one of the courageous lawyers, who had refused to bear any part in the iniquitous trial of the Maid, saw her brought forth from the castle. She was weeping, and seemed much troubled, and he heard her cry, "O Rouen, Rouen, is it here that I must die!" He turned away, and witnessed no more.

It is said there were ten thousand people gathered to see her martyrdom: a sullen leaven of hatred to their English masters in many of their hearts, and undissembled pity and regret for Jeanne on their countenances and in their mouths.

The ecclesiastical judges and civil magistrates already occupied their places. The Cardinal of England was there, and the Bishops of Thourenne

Q

and Noyon.   Most of the doctors and masters were
also present—Fabri, Châtillon, Venderez, De Courcelles, Morrice, Hayton, Gastinel, Marguerie, and a
score besides.   Nicole Midy, that shining light of
Paris University, waited to preach his sermon, to
edify the people by the awful example of the Maid,
and meanwhile the people got by heart the names,
writ large on a tablet near the pile, by which her
judges qualified her.

*Jehanne, qui s'est fait nommer la Pucelle, men-
teresse, pernicieuse abuseresse du peuple, divineresse,
superstitieuse, blasphemeresse de Dieu, présomptueuse,
mal créant de la foi du Jhesuscrist, vantaresse, ydo-
latre, cruelle, dissolue, invocatresse de déables, apostate,
schismatique and hérétique.*

When the guard reached the scaffold with their
prisoner, she was placed by the preacher, and opposite her judges.   Brother Isambard then came
to her, and he and Brother Martin stayed by her,
encouraging and comforting her to the end.   She
hushed her sobs, and stood with the utmost con-
stancy and patience from the moment Midy began
his sermon, taking for his text the words of St.
Paul to the Corinthians—" If one member suffers,
all the members suffer with it," until he concluded
with the formula, "Jeanne, go in peace; the Church
can no longer protect thee, and leaves thee to the
secular power," when, with a gesture of his hand,
he seemed to put her away out of the fold.   Then,

as she fell on her knees, weeping again, to make
her last prayers to God, that arch-hypocrite, the
bishop, took up the word, and said—" Occupy
yourself now with your salvation, Jeanne. Recall
your crimes, that you may be excited to a true contrition, to the penitence necessary for salvation :
and especially give heed to the counsel of the two
brethren who are by you to instruct you."

She did not require his admonition. She poured
forth her heart like one who cries to God out of the
deep that He will not be extreme to mark what is
done amiss. She forgave her enemies, and entreated their forgiveness. She invoked the succour
of her beloved saints ; she saw the perfect light,
and accepted death as her deliverance. To the
last she maintained that her work had been appointed her of God, and none of her revelations
would she deny. When her adversary tempted her
again to lay some dishonour upon Charles, she
answered him with generous courage—" Whether
I have ill-done, or whether I have well-done,
touches not the king ; it was not *he* who counselled me!" And in her prayers she continued
nearly half-an-hour—prayers so touching, true, and
fervent that there was not there a man of heart
so hard but that he wept for her. The Bishop of
Thourenne, who had helped to sell her, was broken
down and sobbing ; big tears rolled over the cheeks
of her wicked judge ; and the proud, bad Car-

dinal of England was seen by many to be staring
through a glassy mist.

She asked for a cross, and an English soldier
who was at the foot of the scaffold, observing that
her request was not promptly granted, made
one of a broken stick he had, and gave it to
her.   She accepted it, thanking him, kissed it, and
put it into her bosom.   Brother Isambard per-
suaded the clerk of St. Saviour's to fetch the
crucifix from the church, that he might have it to
hold up before her in her extremity.   When it was
brought, she took it herself, and kept it closely
embraced, weeping, weeping as if her very life
would flow away in tears, while the Bishop of
Beauvais cleared his countenance, and set himself
to read her sentence before the people.

In his preface to it he said, that from what had
been proved since her abjuration, she had never
abandoned her errors and horrible crimes ; that
with diabolical malice she had assumed a false appearance of penitence, perjuring the holy name of
God, falling into more damnable blasphemies than
before ; which made her relapsed into heresy, and
unworthy of the grace and communion of the
Church, mercifully accorded to her by the former
sentence ; in consequence of which, after ripe deliberation with many learned persons, he and his
colleagues had pronounced her final condemnation.

The said condemnation was addressed to Jeanne

personally, and opened with a dissertation on the
duty of Christian pastors, according to the gospel
of the Inquisition, and concluded by declaring her
a relapsed heretic, a corrupt member: "And as
such, that you may not corrupt others, we declare
you rejected and cut off from the Church, and we
deliver you up to the secular power, praying it to
moderate its judgment with regard to you, and to
spare you death, and mutilation of members."

But by a singular fatality, these Christian pastors
had all the dishonour to themselves of removing
from the Church and the world the noble and devout soul they had toiled so assiduously to betray
to death. The soldiers were growing impatient for
their prey, and one, more brutal than his fellows,
roared out—" Come, you priests, are you going to
make us dine here ?" Immediately two officials
ascended the scaffold; and a voice said hastily—
"Take her away, take her away!" Jeanne made
her reverence to the crowd of priests, begged them
to say all a mass for her, and then committed herself to the two monks. No civil sentence was
given, and the secular power escaped the disgrace
of concurring in an atrocious crime.

When Jeanne descended into the crowd, the
soldiers hurried her with fury to the pile. Their
rage was hideous. The ecclesiastics began to flee,
denouncing the excessive rigour with which the
punishment they had decreed against her was to

be done. The executioner himself was in terror of his task, from the great renown she had, and still more from the cruel way in which he had been bidden to bind her above the wood, so that when the fire was kindled he would not be able to reach her, mercifully to expedite death.

Brother Isambard and Brother Martin mounted the pile with her. The soldiers bade the executioner do his duty, and immediately she was raised and bound to the stake, a mark for ten thousand eyes. High-uplifted there, Jeanne beheld the multitudes at gaze, and the beautiful towers of the city, and conscious of her innocence, she cried—" Oh! Rouen, Rouen, I fear thou wilt have to suffer for my death!"

The soldiers closed round, rank upon rank of loud, excited men. Jeanne had seen their backs often—she saw their faces now. There was the soldier who feared her more than a hundred armed men, and the soldier who feared her more than five hundred armed men, and the soldier who feared her more than all the armies of France, and the soldier who was so bitter against her, he had sworn to bring a brand to her burning, and the soldiers (and they were many) who believed she was no maid, and no woman, but a monstrous *something* of the devil's own making, with only a woman's face.

The executioner set fire to the pile from below, and the grotesque horror of the scene moved

some of the English to laughter. At this moment
came down from his tribunal the Bishop of
Beauvais, with some of the canons of the cathedral, and confronted his victim. What did he
yet hope for? Some womanish plea for mercy?
Some blame of her king, wrung from her by terror?
Some casting-up against her saints, against God
Himself, that they had forsaken her? He got none
of these. She possessed her soul in peace, though
her body trembled at the coming agony, and she
sinned not with her lips. Twice she had warned
him to take heed how he judged her, and now she
warned him to repent that he had judged amiss.
Passing by the cruel instruments, she condemned
the murderous hand that used them, the wicked
head and heart that had plotted her death, and
accomplished it in the name of the Divine Mercy.
Speaking sadly but distinctly, so that all around
heard her, she repeated what she had said to him
in the prison—"Bishop, I die by you. If you had
put me into the hands of the Church, I had never
come here!"

The two brethren, kneeling, weeping, praying by
her, did not perceive the fire creeping up. But she
did, and bade them go down. "And hold high the
crucifix before me, and speak loud enough for me
to hear you until I die," said she : and so was left,
looking up to heaven, calling on Christ and His
saints.

When the fire touched her, she shuddered and cried, "*Water, holy water!*" then "*Jesus! Jesus!*" For a little while, all the air from earth to heaven throbbed with the prayer of her anguish:—"*Jesus! Jesus!*" The eyes of the people were dazzled and dim. Some saw the name of the Redeemer written in the eddying furnace-blast: others saw a white dove hovering in the smoke of her sacrifice.

Brother Martin, standing almost in the draft of the flames, heard her sob with a last sublime effort of faith, bearing her witness to God whom she trusted: "*My voices have not deceived me!*" And then came death, and with great victory delivered her. "JESUS!" with a very loud voice she cried again : and her spirit passed.

For a moment there was silence. Then—"Draw back the fire, and show her *dead* to the people, that none may ever say she has escaped!"

The soldiers stared aghast : hoarse mutterings of indignation rolled through the crowd.

"She was unjustly condemned—unjustly condemned!"

"*Her soul is in the hand of God!*"

When all was over, the Cardinal of England commanded the ashes of the Maid to be cast into the Seine. The executioner finished his work, and then sought the two good monks, to confess himself,—to hear if there could in heaven be pardon for him who had put his hand to the destruction of a creature so holy.

" Her heart, it would not burn, it would not burn, it was full of blood !" said he, marvelling as at a manifest miracle.

And the executioner was not the only penitent. There came to them, by and by, the English soldier who had hated her so marvellously, that he had carried a brand to throw on the pile ; but as he cast it into the fire, Jeanne's last great cry rang over the crowd, and smitten with a terrible repentance, he fell to the earth insensible. Come to himself again, his heart was changed, and he declared that she whom he had persecuted, was a creature of God.

Also, one of the royal secretaries, who had been very violent against her, who had gone exulting to see her die, came away saying— "We are all lost men ; for we have destroyed a saint !"

Clément de Fauquemberque records the event on the register of the parliament of Paris thus :— " The thirtieth day of May, MCCCCXXXI., by trial of the Church, Jeanne, who called herself the Maid, who had been taken in a sally from the city of Compiègne, by the people of Messire Jean of Luxembourg who were with others at the siege of that city, was burnt in the city of Rouen." He then gives the inscriptions on the mitre and on the tablet, adds that Pierre Cauchon, Bishop of Beauvais, pronounced the sentence, and that many notable churchmen of the Duchy of Normandy, and theologians and jurists of the University of Paris, had assisted at the trial. He concludes with a brief prayer for her salvation :—*Deus suæ animæ sit propitius et misericors.*

X.

THE NEWS SPREAD THROUGH CHRISTENDOM.

WHEN the Bishop of Beauvais retired from the Old Market, after the martyrdom of the Maid, his beautiful trial must have looked liked a broken and battered mask, with the devil's face grinning at him through its gaps. Jeanne had publicly charged him as her betrayer; she had publicly averred that if there was error in her deeds, Charles VII. had no part in it; she had maintained the verity of her revelations to her life's end, and she had died like a saint. The populace of Rouen expressed their abhorrence of her judges; it was common fame in the city that she had been unjustly done to death to appease the hate of the English, and " many there were, both there and elsewhere, who said she was a martyr for God."

There was, of course, another opinion also. Some said she had been let live too long; and when the lapse of a few days had taken off men's

nerves the depressing effect of the tragedy, those
for whose profit it had been performed, set themselves to make the best of it. The beautiful trial
had been done with such dexterous adherence to
inquisitorial law, that with skill, its mask might yet
be patched and painted up to look well at a distance
—and that was the momentous business to be accomplished now. The news of the great piece of
championship the King of England had done for
God and the faith, must be spread through Christendom quickly and discreetly, to forestall any
awkward rumours that might get abroad. The
University of Paris had already written to inform
the Pope and the College of Cardinals of its own
zeal in the cause; and it appeared necessary to
the honour of the English government, that letters
should be addressed to the emperors, kings, dukes,
and all the reigning princes of Europe, and to the
prelates, nobles, and cities of France, apprizing
them that the Maid, whose exploits had astonished
the world, and revived the fallen fortunes of Charles
VII., had been put to death in Rouen on a judgment of the Church.

The authentic acts of the trial did not afford
the matter essential to the composition of these
manifestoes. But the bishop was an adept at
manipulating evidence. On the 7th of June, just
a week after Jeanne's death, he summoned to his
house the priests who had visited her in prison on

her last morning—Venderez, Morrice, Loiselleur, De Courcelles, Le Camus, Martin l'Advenu, and Jean Toutmouillé. They each made a statement on oath of what they recollected to have heard her say, and their statements showed that variance, which such witnesses, under such circumstances, might be expected to betray. About Jeanne's confession touching the king's sign, they were of one mind, and they agreed as to her manner of seeing her apparitions, and hearing her *voices*. But what the bishop wanted was a plain certification that she had denied her visions altogether, or else had repudiated them as bad spirits who had deceived her. It was precisely on this point his witnesses differed.

Morrice quoted Jeanne's own words, when questioned of the reality of her apparitions: "*Be they good spirits, or be they evil spirits, they did appear to me.*" De Courcelles quoted her literal words again in her reply to the bishop, challenging her to say whether her *voices* had not deceived her, in promising her deliverance: "*I see that I was deceived.*" Jean Toutmouillé quoted them a third time, in her answer to the judge, when he asked whether, since they had deceived her, she believed them to be good or bad *voices:* "*I do not know! I leave it to you churchmen.*"

In the mouths of Le Camus, Loiselleur, and Venderez, using their own terms, these expressions, drawn from Jeanne in an hour of extremest mental torture, became, that her *voices* had always promised to deliver her out of prison, that now she knew they had deceived her, and therefore she did not any longer believe them to be good *voices*. Martin l'Advenu had not courage to declare her dying words. Le Camus and the abject Loiselleur entered into details, evidently drawn from their compliant imaginations; and the bishop, adopting the worst sense of his witnesses, and amplifying it a little further, found it would sufficiently answer the purpose of his accomplices. Manchon, the notary, was asked to authenticate the document* with his signature. But it testified of things he had not heard; he might well doubt of its accuracy; for it had all the air of having been got up to calumniate Jeanne, and he refused. Her death had completely unmanned him; part of his wages he had spent to purchase a missal to pray for her; and, in his own heart, believing her good and true, he would not lend himself to dishonour her memory. His conscience was, perhaps, not quite clear towards her before.

The bishop dispensed with the notary's signature, and added this very suspicious document to the body of acts and minutes of the trial which Manchon and his colleague, Boisguillaume, had

---

* Some French writers treat the whole piece as a forgery. But it bears more the appearance of ingeniously mingled fact and fiction.

authenticated. The day after the witnesses were examined, the manifesto to be circulated amongst the sovereigns of Europe was drawn up. It consisted of a declamation on the danger of errors in the faith and of false prophets, with an epitome of the Maid's life and conversation from the point of view of her king's adversaries, and a very inexact outline of the trial, and the judgments pronounced against her. It wound up with an exhortation to all princes that they would follow the example of the English king in preventing, by severe punishments, the mischiefs which attend on false prophets and their teachings.

This letter was dated from Rouen on the 8th of June, and on the 12th, before the manifesto destined for France could be issued, either the evil conscience of the judges, or the fear they were in of being called to account for their conduct in the Maid's trial, made them require of the English government a sort of safeguard, or letter of guarantee, that they should have its protection and defence if they were meddled with. This curious document shows very significantly in what light the matter was viewed by some in Rouen, and what might come of it, if more powerful and independent men than these few provincial dissentients took it up. The English government did not lose the opportunity of laying the onus of the work on the broad back of the University of Paris, which had

advised it, and helped it to its notable end.   Thus,
in effect, runs the letter:—

" Henry, by the grace of God, King of France
and England, to all who shall see these present
letters, greeting.   Some time ago, having been
required by our well-beloved daughter, the University of Paris, to give up to the Church that
woman called Jeanne the Maid, who had been
taken in arms in the diocese of Beauvais, as notoriously defamed of having sown, in divers places
of our kingdom of France, great errors . . . having
also been summoned by our faithful counsellor, the
Bishop of Beauvais, her judge-ordinary, . . . we,
like a true Catholic, . . . not desiring to do anything that might be in any way prejudicial to the
holy Inquisition of our holy faith, . . . and desiring
to prefer it to every other means of secular and
temporal justice, rendering to each its due, did give
and deliver the woman to her judge-ordinary, . . .
to have justice done, . . . who joined with him the
vicar of the inquisitor, . . . and, after trial, gave
final sentence against her as a heretic and relapsed,
. . . abandoning her to our secular justice, . . . by
which she was condemned to be burnt, and was
thus executed.   As, perchance, there may be some
who approved of her errors and iniquities, and
others who for hatred or vengeance may seek to
disturb the true judgments of our mother, holy

Church, and to bring before our holy father the
Pope, or the General Council, the reverend father
in God, the vicar, doctors, masters, clerks, promoters,
advocates, counsellors, notaries or others who were
engaged in the trial: WE, as protector and defender
of our holy Catholic faith, will support and defend
them, . . . and all they have said and pronounced.
. . . WE PROMISE, on the word of a king, that if
any of these persons, of whatever state, dignity,
pre-eminent degree or authority they may be, are
cited in cause before the Pope or General Council,
or commissioners deputed by them, we will aid and
defend them in judgment and out, . . . at our own
cost and expense . . . And we command all our
ambassadors and envoys . . . at the court of Rome
and at the General Council, . . . all bishops, prelates, doctors and masters, our subjects, . . . if any
of the aforesaid be cited before the Pope or Council, . . . that, in our name, they instantly undertake
their cause and defence . . . and we require all
kings, princes, and lords, our allies, that they give
them counsel, help, and assistance, in every possible manner, without difficulty or delay. In witness
of which we have set our seal to these presents.
Given at Rouen the twelfth day of June, the year
of grace MCCCCXXXI. and of our reign the ninth.
Et in plica: On the part of the KING, in the
presence of his Great Council, at which were the
Lord Cardinal of England, you, the Bishops of

Beauvais, Noyon, and Norwich ; the Earls of War-
wich and Stafford ; the Abbots of Feçamp and
Mont-Saint-Michel ; and the Lords Cromwell,
Tipetot, and Saint-Père, and several others. *Sic
signatum*, CALOT."

This guarantee, which was a condemnation of
those who needed it, was *not* consigned to the mass
of documents belonging to the trial, materially as
it concerned them ; but when the trial was revised,
and its sentences reversed five-and-twenty years
after, it was in the hands of those commissioned by
the Pope to render tardy justice to the memory of
the Maid and her cowardly pursuers.

The manifesto circulated amongst the prelates,
nobles, and cities of France, had in view the direct
object of defaming Jeanne, and of drawing away
from Charles VII. his subjects who, by her means,
had been restored to their lawful allegiance. Its
lying audacity would be almost ludicrous, if it were
not so abominable, and if it had not exercised so
pernicious an influence on popular opinion as it
evidently did for many years. The names of the
Inquisition and the University carried much weight,
and French France was struck dumb by the authority that condemned the Maid. The document was
very long, and ran to the following effect :—

"It is everywhere notorious enough how that
woman who called herself *Jeanne the Maid*, divin-

eress, did more than two years ago, against the
Divine law, . . . clothe herself as a man, . . . and
in this condition joined our capital enemy, to
whom, and to those of his party, clergy, nobles, and
commons, she gave it to be understood that she
was sent on the part of God, . . . by which, with
the hope of future victories, she turned many hearts
of men and women from the way of truth, convert-
ing them to fables and lies. She arrayed herself in
arms fit for knights and esquires, raised her standard, and with outrageous pride and presumption
asked to have and to bear the very noble and
excellent arms of France ; which, in part, she did
obtain, and carried them in several conflicts and
assaults. . . . In this state she took the field, leading men-at-arms and archers . . . to shed human
blood, . . . making commotion amongst the people,
. . . inciting them to rebellion, . . . disturbing all
true peace, and renewing mortal war, . . . suffering
herself to be adored and revered as a sainted
woman, . . . and doing damnably in divers other
ways, too long to be detailed. But the Divine
power, having pity on His loyal people, did not
leave them in peril, . . . but of His great mercy and
clemency, permitted this woman to be taken before Compiègne, and put into our obedience. And
because the bishop of the diocese where she had
been taken required it of us, . . . and in reverence
for our holy mother Church, whose ordinances we

would always put before our own will, . . . we
caused her to be given up to him for trial, . . .
without desiring the officers of our secular justice
to take any vengeance on her, as we reasonably
and lawfully might have done, considering the great
mischiefs, the horrible homicides, the detestable
cruelties, and other innumerable evils, which she had
committed against our loyal and obedient people.
The bishop, in conjunction with the inquisitor of
errors and heresies, called on masters and doctors
in theology and canon law, and with much solemnity and gravity began the trial of the said Jeanne.
And after they had for several days interrogated
her, . . . her confessions and assertions were maturely examined by the masters and doctors, and
generally by all the Faculties of our dear and well-
beloved daughter, the University of Paris, to whom
her confessions and assertions were sent. On their
opinion, the judges found her superstitious, diviner-
ess, idolatress, invocatress of devils, a blasphemer of
God and His saints, schismatic, and erring much in
the faith of Jesus Christ. To reduce and bring her
back to the unity and communion of our holy
mother Church, to purge her from such horrible,
detestable, and pernicious crimes and sins, and to
heal and save her soul from everlasting damnation,
she was often mildly and charitably admonished.
. . . But the perilous spirit of pride and outrageous presumption . . . so occupied and held in

its bonds the heart of the woman, that by no whole-
some counsel or doctrine, or any gentle exhortation,
could it be softened or humbled ; but often she
boasted that everything she had done was well
done, and by the command of God. . . . And
what was worse, she would acknowledge no judge
on earth but God only, . . . refusing the judgment
of our holy father the Pope, of the General Council,
and the Universal Church militant. Therefore the
ecclesiastical judges, seeing her so long hardened
and obstinate, brought her forth before the clergy
and people, assembled in great multitude, in whose
presence her crimes and errors were solemnly set
forth by a notable master in theology, . . . and she
was again charitably admonished to return to the
union of holy Church, and to correct her errors,
in which she still persisted. . . . Considering this,
the judges proceeded to pronounce the sentence
against her, as in such cases ordained by the law.
. . . But before it was done, her courage began
to fail, and she said she would return to holy
Church. This joyfully the judges and clergy heard,
and benignly received her, hoping by this means
to rescue her body and soul from perdition. . . .
These her errors and detestable crimes she revoked
with her mouth, and publicly abjured, signing with
her own hand the schedule of revocation and abjuration. And our pitying mother, holy Church,
rejoicing over the penitent sinner, desiring to bring

back the sheep gone astray in the wilderness, for
salutary penance condemned her to the castle.
But in a very short while, the fire of her pride was
blown into pestilential flames by the breath of the
enemy, and the unfortunate woman relapsed into
her errors and false frenzies, which she had abjured.
For these things, according as the institutions of
holy Church ordain, that she might not henceforward contaminate the other members of Jesus
Christ, . . . she was abandoned to the secular
power, which instantly condemned her to be burnt.
Seeing her end approach, she plainly knew and
confessed that the spirits which she said appeared
to her, were bad and lying, and that the promise
these spirits had often made to deliver her was
false ; and thus she confessed herself to have been
mocked and deceived by them.

" Here is the end of these things: here is the
end of that woman which we signify to you,
reverend father in God, that you may be truly
informed of this matter; and that in all places of
your diocese, where it may seem good to you, public
sermons on it may be made, for the edification of
the Christian people, who have been long deceived
by this woman ; . . . that they may not presume
to believe lightly in such errors and perilous superstitions ; . . . lest the venom of false faith contaminate them ; which Jesus Christ, in His mercy,
prevent. And be you, as His ministers, to whom

it belongs, diligent in repressing and punishing the wiles and foolish boldness of all men suspect of such errors.

" Given in our city of Rouen, the xxviii. day of June."

Thus was the news of the Maid's cruel martyrdom disseminated through France. When it came to Charles, the old chronicler, Pierre Sala, says: " *Il fut moult doulent, mais rémedier n'y peut*"—the only notice there is of his feelings any where: " He was much grieved, but he could not remedy it."

When it came to Domremy, it broke the heart of Jeanne's father, and he died. Her eldest brother soon followed him; but Pierre and Jean lived on, and fought through the disgrace; and her poor mother, pensioned by the city of Orleans, survived to see her name restored to honour, and a cross erected to her perpetual memory on the spot where she died. But many changes were to happen before that.

Some prelates complied with the request of the English King, and caused sermons to be made on Jeanne. There was one preached in Paris, about as true to fact as the royal manifesto. The Dominican who delivered it, gave out that the penitent, on her abjuration, had been only condemned to four years' imprisonment. In Rouen, however, the impression produced by her victorious death did not wear off. It began to seem, too, as if the judgment of God were coming on her persecutors. Jean d'Estivet, her bitter reviler, was found dead on a dunghill, outside the city gates. Nicolás Loiselleur, her infamous betrayer, had been forced to fly. He went to Bâle, and there one day, in a church, he suddenly dropped down, and expired. But the Bishop of Beauvais was not a man to be daunted by superstitious previsions. He neither feared God nor regarded man, and was only intent on putting a stop to the mischievous talk which impugned the fairness of his beautiful trial, and threatened to weaken the influence of its notable conclusion. Finding it did not die away of itself, but rather increased, he determined to make an example of the first offender he could lawfully lay hold of, and to terrify Rouen into silence.

The scapegoat was a too convivial monk, Pierre Bosquier, who, in an indiscreet after-dinner mood, declared that Jeanne the Maid had been ill-tried and ill-judged by everybody who had taken any part in the cause against her. He was denounced to the bishop as a favourer of her heresies, and though he pleaded that he spoke in his cups, the prelate did not excuse him. He was condemned to beg pardon on his knees, and to be imprisoned on bread and water in the house of the Dominican friars from the date of his sentence, August 8th, to the Easter Sunday following. From that time, for many years forward, the Maid's trial became an event of which people in Rouen did not like to talk.

After the lapse of some months, Thomas de Courcelles was chosen to translate into Latin, and to draw up in the form of letters-patent, proceeding from Pierre Cauchon, the bishop, and Jean Lemaître, the inquisitor, all the acts and interrogatories on the trial; which thus read as a long narrative put into the mouths of the two judges. Manchon assisted him, and made three complete copies of the whole. The translation of the interrogatories, as recorded on the notary's minutes, was faithful; but already the conscience of De Courcelles had begun to tell him that there was shame in the deed at which he had worked so zealously; and he tried to screen himself, by omitting to mention his own name as that of the counsellor who read the Act of Accusation; and by suppressing the votes of the assessors on the matter of applying the torture to Jeanne, when he was one of three (out of twelve) who advised it. He exercised the same discretion for all the members of the council, in which the XII. Articles were compiled. Copies of Manchon's original notes, however, remained to betray his part in the two former instances; but the absence of the notary from the council on the Articles preserved the secret of the men who composed it.

XI.

THE EXPIATION.

RELIEVED from the terror of Jeanne d'Arc and her witchcrafts, the English returned with new heart to the war. But their labour in France was henceforward only like the vain toil of an ebbing tide. There was the little flux that seemed to gain on the sand, and the reflux which imperceptibly retired; but by rocks rising out of the level at intervals, was marked the lost ground, and the space from which the flood had gone down.

In the harvest they defeated the royal army near Beauvais, and made prisoner, amongst others, of Poton de Saintrailles, and also of the wretched shepherd boy who had come out of the mountains of Gévaudun to rival the Maid. They evidenced their sense of his insignificance by putting him into a sack, and tossing him into the river. This

success was followed by counterbalancing disasters, and towards the close of the year, as a means
of confirming the English power, Henry VI. was
carried to Paris, and crowned King of France; but
with such poor splendour and festivity, that the
populace ridiculed the whole affair, and said a
citizen marrying his daughter would have done it
more handsomely.

But already upon the name and fame of Jeanne
d'Arc was falling the silence of public infamy. In
an Assembly of the Three Estates held at Blois in
1433, when thanks were returned to God for the
miraculous successes of Charles VII., the honour of
them was ascribed to "a little company of valiant
men to whom He had given courage to undertake
the cause"—of the Maid no mention at all. The
same reticence appears in other public acts and
documents. But in the household of the Duke of
Alençon, and perhaps in many more, she was
secretly revered. Louis de Cagny, writing the
chronicle of the family, whose servitor he was for
forty years, records it to his master's honour that
Jeanne d'Arc preferred him above all her companions-in-arms; and in reciting the great things
she did for France, he says emphatically that she
would have done yet greater if the king and those
men in his confidence who governed all, had but
conducted themselves well towards her. In Metz,
Jean de Novelonpont's city, it was more openly

proclaimed that Georges de la Trémouille was the
cause of her death ; and the soldiers, who remembered her with affection, declared that for jealousy
some of their captains had betrayed her.   Guillaume de Flavy, governor of Compiègne, who
achieved an infamous reputation by and by, was
believed, on the testimony of his wife, who had con-
nived at his murder, to have literally sold the Maid
to Jean of Luxembourg ; but there is no contem-
porary evidence of such a treason, and the witnesses of her capture all speak of it merely as one
of the casualties common to war.

The sanguinary quarrel went on with fluctuating
fortunes until 1435.   The people would not endure
the yoke, and the Duke of Bedford would not take
it off.   Peace seemed still as far as ever from the
troubled nation, when all the powers of Europe
agreed to intervene, and to compel the contending
princes to give it rest.   A great congress met at
Arras in August; but Bedford withdrew from it
the moment he became aware the Treaty of
Troyes would not be allowed to stand.   He
retired to Rouen, and died there in the castle, a
few weeks after—an able statesman who had
inherited a bad quarrel, and had wasted his life
in fighting for it, while England was verging
downwards to miseries and disasters and civil wars,
hardly less cruel than those which had so long
desolated France.

The death of his ally set the Duke of Burgundy free from many irksome obligations. The papal legates absolved him from his vow of vengeance against Charles, and a treaty of reconciliation was signed between them. The first fruits of this treaty to the king was the recovery of Paris. In May 1436, the citizens opened their gates to the royal force under the command of the Constable de Richemont and the Count of Dunois. The English garrison capitulated on honourable terms, marched round the ramparts once, and then marched out of the city, and embarking on the Seine, went their way to Rouen—thus abandoning a greater gage than they had abandoned before Orleans, as Jeanne d'Arc had promised them they should do before seven years were at an end.

Another reverse now ensued, and legend began to take possession of the Maid's name. It was precisely in the month of May 1436, when Paris was restored to the obedience of Charles, that there flew abroad a rumour that Jeanne was alive again—that she had never been burned at Rouen—that she had escaped the fire by her miraculous holiness. Orleans had kept the anniversary of her martyrdom yearly in the church of Saint-Sanxon, burning tapers, with shields of her arms attached to them, and a great flambeaux of wax, while eight monks of the four mendicant orders sang masses

for the repose of her soul. Sensible men saw
through the imposture that was attempted to be
palmed off on France; but to the simple, credulous
people, who in her lifetime had adored Jeanne,
there was nothing past belief in the new wonder,
and they readily opened their ears to receive it.

The woman claiming to be the Maid first appeared at Metz. She afterwards passed some time
at the court of Luxembourg, and thence addressed
letters to Charles VII. at Loches, and to Orleans.
The city sent her a reply by its herald-at-arms, and
Pierre and Jean des Lys made a journey to Metz
to see her. She had Jeanne's skill at arms and her
grace on horseback, and must also have had a
strong personal likeness to her; for the Maid's
brothers acknowledged her as their sister at the
time, and several other persons were sure she was
the famous deliverer of Orleans. At Metz she
married a knight, Robert des Armoises, and set-
tling there in his house, bore him two sons.

Her next appearance was at Orleans itself, in
1439, as Jeanne des Armoises, and she was several
times presented with gifts of wine, and at her departure with a sum of money. She had the conduct of troops in Poitou, and there achieved some
repute. But the popular credulity was not shared
by the court, and Charles, apparently in the design
of unmasking the pretender, ordered her to be
brought before him. He had been wounded in the

foot, and wore a soft boot, of which, by some in her interest, she had been warned, that she might know him amongst his gentlemen. He was in the garden, under a large arbour, when she arrived, and by Charles's desire, one of the nobles advanced to meet her, feigning himself the king. But she passed him by, and went straight to the true king, as the true Jeanne had done. Charles bowed to her, and said graciously:—" Maid, in God's name who knows the secret that is between you and me, you are very welcome back!" The woman, frightened by this allusion to a matter of which she was ignorant, fell on her knees, and confessed her imposture.

The report of her was still, however, kept alive, and in 1440 the University and Parliament of Paris had her brought to the capital, whether she would or no, and she was exhibited to the people standing on a pedestal of stone in the great court of the palace. Here she was sermonised, and her life and adventures set forth by the preacher. He said that she was married to a knight, and that she had two sons ; that by misadventure she had almost killed her mother, and had fled to Rome disguised as a man ; that she had taken part in the wars of Pope Eugenius in Germany and Italy, and had twice committed homicide in them. After her exposure, she was let go, and the last authentic notice of her is in a document transferring the troops she had commanded in Poitou to a Gascon gentleman. It bears date 1441.   She then vanished into obscurity, and the romancers, taking up her half fabulous exploits, interwove them with the well-known victories of Jeanne the Maid, and out of the two constructed a heroine whose adventures rivalled those of the Arthurian or Carolingian knights.

Thus had ten years' space sufficed to develop Jeanne d'Arc into an almost mythical personage. Ten years more saw the investigation begun which restored her fame to its natural and noble truth, and confirmed it for ever.

In 1440 the Duke of Orleans was ransomed out of captivity in England, after an exile of five-and-thirty years.   The war between French and English languished on till 1444, when they made a truce, which was again broken in 1448.   Charles VII. then sent an army into Normandy, where the Duke of Somerset was governor, and in the October of the following year, Rouen opened its gates to the Count of Dunois.   On the 11th of November, the king himself entered the city of the Maid's martyrdom ; and early in the ensuing year he gave letters of commission to his counsellor Guillaume Bouillé, a doctor of divinity, to inquire into the true circumstances of her death.

Age had improved Charles's character.   He and all France could now look back without prejudice, and see how opportunely Jeanne d'Arc had suc-

coured the monarchy; how she had, indeed, saved
it from a fall which had been judged inevitable.
The beauty of her character and the disinterested-
ness of her brief career could be viewed at last,
without jealousy, without distrust. Charles, in her
lifetime, had never heartily believed in her, as too
well she had experienced; but he believed in her
now. Those who had done her faithful service, he
promoted to honour; Jean de Metz he ennobled,
Jean d'Aulon he made seneschal of Beaucaire.
Death had reaped long since her worst enemies,
and he sought no revenges—remembering, perhaps, that Jeanne was one to whom revenges had
never been sweet. But his conscience, tardily
awakened, let him rest no more until he had done
all in the power of a king to repair former ingra-
titudes, and to restore her good fame.

Seven witnesses were examined on this occasion;
Jean Beaupère, Martin l'Advenu, Brother Isambard
de la Pierre, Manchon, Massieu, Toutmouillé, and
Guillaume Duval. Beaupère, now an old man of
seventy, held boldly to his original opinions: that
Jeanne's apparitions were not supernatural, and that
as for her innocence, she was very subtle, though
he never heard her say anything to lead him to
think her corrupt. He could not speak of her
death, for he left Rouen to go to Bâle the Monday
before, and he did not hear of her condemnation
until some time after, when he was at Lisle in Flan-

ders. But those who could speak of her death spared
Charles none of the cruel details.   Massieu let him
hear what she suffered at the hands of her gaolers;
Martin l'Advenu told him how, on the morning of
her martyrdom, he had administered to her the
sacraments of penance and the Eucharist, and how
she had received them with such tears and devotion
as he could not describe ; Brother Isambard told
him that, when the Church abandoned her, she still
clung to the Cross ; and, concluded he, with words
of comfort equal to such sorrows : " In rendering
up her spirit, and inclining her head, she uttered
the holy name of JESUS, in sign that she was fervent in the faith of God, as we read of St. Ignatius
and many other martyrs."

The testimony of these witnesses had impeached
the lawfulness of the trial at many points, notwithstanding the imposing front of authority and fairness that the Bishop of Beauvais had contrived to
make it present to the world.   He had died suddenly ten years before, while his valet was trimming
his beard, and his bones rested under a fine tomb
in the cathedral of Lisieux, to which see he had been
translated by the English when it was found that
the Pope would not adopt their recommendation
to make him Archbishop of Rouen.   He was therefore beyond reach of account and explanation; but
Charles went diligently to work to upset the beautiful trial on which the wicked prelate had glorified
himself.

One of Manchon's copies of the Latin edition by Thomas de Courcelles, had been sent to Rome, and Theodorus Leliis, auditor in the papal court of appeals, the most famous canonist of the fifteenth century, made a summary of Jeanne's answers under twelve heads, to be compared with the XII. Articles, and a list of points of law to be submitted to consultants. Amongst the principal opinions given were those of Paul Pontanus, an advocate of the apostolical consistory, and Jean Bréhal, inquisi- tor-general in the kingdom of France. By all, the trial was declared to be full of vices of form and procedure ; and the XII. Articles were qualified as deceitful, imperfect, and lying.

In 1452, Cardinal d'Estouteville, legate from Rome, by Charles's desire, received the testimony of seve- ral witnesses in Rouen, and on his departure, dele- gated Philippe de Rose, treasurer of the cathedral, to continue the investigation. The chief of those who had given evidence before, were called again, and as many assessors as remained in Normandy. Jean Fabri, now Bishop of Demetriade, Marguerie, the Prior of Longueville, and Bouchier, came for- ward, with Houppeville, Taquel, Cusquel, and several citizens and priests of Rouen who had not been on the trial. Every one—without apparently perceiving what a terrible verdict they were passing on the French ecclesiastics who had condemned the Maid—either admitted or alleged in their excuse that whatever had been done, had been done for

fear or favour of the English. Only Brother Isambard was found with courage enough to adduce the
better plea, that the judges had sufficiently observed the forms of inquisitorial law. One divine,
Thomas Marie, with an unconscious double-edged
ambiguity, declared in his evidence that if Jeanne
had belonged to the English, they would not have
ill-used her, but would hardly have known how to
honour her enough.

True. If Jeanne had delivered half England
from a foreign invader, that half would not have
abandoned her to her enemies ; and the whole
island would not have furnished a tribunal of fifty or
sixty covetous, time-serving, perplexed, cowardly
ecclesiastics of her own blood, to betray her to a
shameful and agonising death for their gratification.
The English lord, who wished aloud in the hall that
she were English, represented that spirit of fair-
play inherent in his nation, which, much as she was
feared, hated, and execrated at the time of her capture, might have ended in respecting her as an
honourable foe, if the clergy, charged with her
trial, had laboured to prove her innocence with a
tithe of the ardour they showed in putting all her
words and deeds under the malign and baleful medium through which the superstitious soldiery of
England and Burgundy had learnt to regard her.

The result of the investigations at Rouen was
·gradually noised abroad, at Rome and elsewhere,

and others besides Charles began to consider it
only a matter of common justice that Jeanne
d'Arc's memory should be relieved from the infamous condemnation that weighed upon it. But
it was no easy thing to obtain a reversal of a judgment of the Church, and it was not until 1455 that
the necessary authority for a formal revision of the
trial was granted by Pope Calixtus III. ; and then
it.was not granted on the petition of the king, but on
the petition of the mother and two surviving brothers of the Maid, Isabelle, Pierre, and Jean d'Arc.

The papal brief was addressed to the Archbishop
of Rheims, the Bishops of Paris and Coutances, and
the grand inquisitor, who were charged to hear
both sides, and to pronounce according to justice.
On the 17th of November these commissioners held
a solemn public audience in the hall of the episcopal
palace in Paris, to receive the demand of the petitioners. A crowd of prelates, abbots, officials from
various dioceses, doctors, masters, and spectators of
all ranks filled the hall, drawn together by the importance and notoriety of the case. When all were
assembled, a mournful procession entered—the poor
old peasant mother of the famous Maid, supported
by her sons, and followed by her advocate, Master
Maugier, and a file of kindred and of divines
who had espoused her cause. She held a piece of
paper in her hand, and speaking for herself, she
made her complaint, broken with tears and sobs.

She was, she said, the mother of Jeanne d'Arc, whom she had brought up in the fear of God, and the traditions of the Church, according to her age and station, which was to live in the meadows and the fields. Her daughter went to church, confessed and communicated often, and fasted on the days prescribed. She had never thought or meditated anything against the faith; nevertheless her enemies, in contempt of the king under whom she lived, had accused her of errors in the faith; and without lawful authority, and in defiance of her tacit and express appeals, had imputed to her false crimes, and had subjected her to a death of irreparable infamy for her and her family.

When Isabelle d'Arc had made her plea, Master Maugier read the petition of herself and her sons, formally impugning the legality of the trial. The commissioners then retired for a while into another apartment to converse with the poor mother apart, and returning presently to the hall of audience, ordered the brief of Pope Calixtus to be publicly read. Maugier then had leave to speak briefly, and he proceeded to set forth that the only persons attacked by the charge of the petitioners were the judges, Pierre Cauchon, Bishop of Beauvais, and Jean Lemaître, inquisitor of the faith, and the promoter, Jean d'Estivet—three dead men; the assessors and consultants having been led into error by the XII. Articles, were not to be accounted responsible for the condemnation they had founded on them.

This announcement that the new trial aimed only at restoring the honour of Jeanne and her family, not at punishing her betrayers, tranquillized the anxieties of the University of Paris, and of others who had been zealous in her prosecution. The judges at once issued their preliminary orders, citing all who had any knowledge of the first cause to appear on the 12th of December, before the court in the city of Rouen, and all who had any acts and documents relating to it, to produce them. The heirs and representatives of Pierre Cauchon, Jean Lemaître, and Jean d'Estivet were also cited to defend their memory, the citations being publicly affixed on the doors of the great churches of Paris, Beauvais, and Rouen; but the heirs of Pierre Cauchon excused themselves from defending him whom the martyred Maid had condemned, and no representatives of the others could be found.

This second trial is very long and complex, but the examinations of the crowd of witnesses who testified on oath to the circumstances of Jeanne d'Arc's life, from her birth to her death, have a deep and permanent interest. They seem to step forth, for a minute or two, living upon the page— Haumette and Mangète telling how good Jeanne was, and how they loved her; Gerard d'Epinal describing the Beautiful May; Simon Musnier de-

tailing an illness he had when a little lad, and how
tenderly Jeanne nursed him; Katherine Royer,
with her story of how the girl wearied to be gone
to the Dauphin; and Jean de Metz and Bertrand
de Poulangy narrating their journey with her into
France. Then come the Count of Dunois and
Raoul de Gaucourt, a veteran of eighty-five, with
a throng of citizens of Orleans, recounting how the
siege was raised; then the Duke of Alençon, Louis
de Contes, Margaret de Bouligny, and Jean Pas-
querel, telling how brave, devout, and pure Jeanne
was—the last expressing his surprise that so many
wise and learned doctors as sat on her trial at
Rouen could have betrayed to death such a simple
Christian; one who, not for the world, would wilfully have offended God. Thomas de Courcelles
passes through a very bad hour,—a man renowned
for learning, piety, and probity, protesting on his
honour, and on his conscience, that he never said
Jeanne was a heretic, save on the condition that she
would not submit to the Church: denying here, ex-
tenuating there, and being confronted with his own
handwriting, to convict him of an evasive memory.
Jacques Tiphaine and Guillaume de la Chambre
have their say about Jeanne's sickness in prison, and
the witnesses of Rouen come forward with recollec-
tions of her trial and death. The last deposition,
and the fullest, is that of Jean d'Aulon, to whom the
Archbishop of Rheims wrote when the rest had been
received, and reports of them sent to Rome :—

"*To my very dear lord and brother, Jean d'Aulon,
councillor of the king and seneschal of Beaucaire.*

" My very dear lord and brother, . . . since I
was at Saint-Porsain with the king, I wrote to you
of the trial made against Jeanne the Maid, by the
English, who maintained that she was a sorceress,
heretic, and invocatress of devils, and that by this
means the king recovered his kingdom; and thus
they held the king, and all who had served him,
heretic. And because of her life, conversation, and
government, you know much and well, I beg that
you will write to me all you do know of her, signed
by two apostolical notaries and an inquisitor of the
faith, for I have a bull to revoke all that her enemies did on that trial.

" Written at Paris, the xx. day of April (1456.)

" THE ARCHBISHOP AND DUKE OF RHEIMS."

The reply to this letter was a record of the
Maid's active career while Jean d'Aulon was her
guardian and constant attendant, up to the date of
the siege of La Charité. It is conjectured that the
depositions of the witnesses were pruned of any
matter not essential to Jeanne's clearance, which
would have condemned or cast a slur on other
persons. The deposition of D'Aulon is one which
betrays signs of such curtailment, and it is the
more probable, because, on the evidence of Louis
de Cagny, the Duke of Alençon's steward, it

appears that the faithful knight continued in her service long after the period where it stops; that he was indeed captured with her at Compiègne, and went with her to Beaulieu.

The witnesses of Jeanne's military exploits—lords and captains, courtiers, soldiers, citizens, and women—all concur in ascribing to her great gifts of nature, great simplicity of heart, and some special guidance of God, which they call *inspiration.* The soldiers are said to have trusted her not for that only, but for the more homely reason that she was so careful and industrious in providing for their common wants, that they suffered fewer neglects and privations when she was with the army, than at other times. In the camp and out of it, her life was universally allowed to have been circumspect, devout, and chaste: "a beautiful life, and it would be impossible for a man to utter one word against her."

After taking the opinions of many great doctors and lawyers, the petitioners for the reversal of Jeanne's condemnation based their final demand on the following grounds :—That the judges were incompetent, Jeanne not having lived in the diocese of Beauvais, or committed there any of the crimes imputed to her. That for reasons more than sufficient, she had challenged and objected to the bishop, and had formally demanded to be sent to the Pope. That she was a minor, and yet no counsel had been given her. That she had been wilfully betrayed into error by perfidious, deceitful, and criminal artifices. That it was not for her judges, or even for the Church itself, to pronounce on her revelations, but for God only; that there was cause to believe hers were divine, because she was pure, humble, and pious; she sought no worldly reward, but her salvation alone; her visions, the first terror over, were attended with holy joy; her *voices* taught her nothing but what was good; and she died a perfect Christian, in the midst of the flames, never ceasing to invoke the Lord Jesus until her spirit was released. That she wore her man's dress to obey a divine command, and that her resumption of it, after she had put it off, could not be heresy. That her parents had forgiven her departure from them without leave; that she had wished to save her life, and not to lose it, in trying to escape from Beaurevoir; and that her fiction of the crown given to the king was like that of Abraham with regard to Sarah, and could not, in any light, be a crime for justice to punish. That she never pretended to be sure she had not sinned mortally; that she had not lied in saying she should be delivered from prison, but had not plainly understood all she herself quoted as what her *voices* said to her of her martyrdom. That when she was properly instructed in the distinction between the Church triumphant and the Church militant, she made due submission, in spite

of the unworthy tricks employed to turn her from
it ; and that the XII. Articles were falsely drawn
up for the express purpose of deceiving the assessors and consultants. Jeanne's good life, and the
notorious partiality of her judges, were referred to,
with the opinions of the doctors, to wind up.

The whole case was recapitulated by the papal
commissioners, and Jean Bréhal, the grand inquisitor, himself wrote the results ; which present a
long series of the motives that prevailed with the
judges of the revision, and prove with what care
and scruples they accomplished their task.

The first chapter is a dissertation on Jeanne's
visions, favourable to their reality ; her revelations
are treated as legitimate, because she was devout
and pure, and France was in great need of succour
from Heaven when she came. With regard to her
predictions, it is concluded that it was not possible
for her tó have invented what she foretold. The
spirits that showed themselves to her are presumed
to have been good ; for all she did and said with
regard to them breathed a fervent piety. Further
on, she is cleared of infractions of Divine law, in
quitting her parents and dressing as a man, by the
motives that influenced her, and the great advan-
tages to her country that resulted. She is justified
from her imputed errors in the faith by the fair
comparison of all her own words, purposely confused and divided by her adversaries ; and is allowed

to have actually submitted to the Church. She is exculpated entirely from the crime of relapse, because her abjuration was extorted by terror, and was imperfectly understood ; because she was re-committed to the custody of a licentious military guard ; because in her own soul she believed her apparitions to be good spirits ; and she was, in fact, delivered from the prison of her body by the most Christian death.

The second chapter concerns the form of the trial. The Bishop of Beauvais is declared incompetent as her judge because he was not her Ordinary, and because of his corrupt partiality against her. Her hard usage in prison is adduced as nullifying the procedure, by troubling her mind, and embarrassing her in her defence. The vice-inquisitor is said to have acted with reluctance, and through fear. The assessors, her pretended defenders, those who exhorted her, those who gave her the monitions, those who preached to her, are all declared to have used means more fit to injure than to help her, seeing that the counsel necessary to her was never given. The crimes and errors of those who deliberated in the cause, and consulted on the XII. Articles, are not spared ; and the trial is finally concluded to be null, and the judgment unjust.

The whole was first published and discussed in Paris ; and on the 7th of July 1456, the Archbishop of Rheims, the Bishops of Paris and Coutances, and the grand inquisitor, gave their sentence in the chapel of the archiepiscopal palace at Rouen. The mother of Jeanne had obtained leave to appear by proxy, but her brothers, Pierre and Jean, were present, and fourteen witnesses—Jean Fabri and Martin l'Advenu amongst them. The Archbishop of Rheims was spokesman, and after passing in review briefly the motives and conclusions of the revisers of the trial, he went on thus :—

" Considering the admirable deliverance of the city of Orleans, the conduct of the king to Rheims, his coronation in that city, and the attendant circumstances :—having implored the aid of Heaven, that our judgment may emanate from God himself, who is the only true Judge, and the only one knowing the reality of those revelations ; of that God whose spirit breathes where He lists, who chooses sometimes the weak to confound the mighty, and never abandons those who hope in Him, but succours them in all sorrow and tribulation : having maturely deliberated on the preparation and decision of the case, . . . we decide that the deeds of the Maid are worthy of admiration, rather than of condemnation ; that all done against her was vicious in form and substance; that it is difficult to judge of revelations, since St. Paul himself, speaking of his own, says, that he knows not whether his soul was in the body or out of the body when he received them, and refers himself to God, who alone can know . . .

The XII. Articles we declare to have been un-
faithfully, wickedly, calumniously, fraudulently,
and maliciously extracted from the confessions of
Jeanne; . . . and as false and full of deceit, we condemn them to be judicially torn. . . . The two
judgments against her, by the first of which she
was sentenced to perpetual prison, and by the
second to death as relapsed, . . . we pronounce
null and invalid. In consequence, Jeanne, the
petitioners, and their kindred, we declare to have
incurred therefrom no blot of infamy, of which in
every event they are entirely cleared.

" This our judgment shall be solemnly published
in the city of Rouen. There shall be made, besides,
two solemn processions : the first to the cemetery
of Saint-Ouen, where passed the scene of the false
abjuration ; the second, on the day following, to
the very place where Jeanne d'Arc was cruelly and
horribly burnt and suffocated by fire. There shall
be in both places a public sermon. And on the
place of her execution there shall be raised a cross
to her perpetual memory.

"Finally, in every city of the kingdom, and in
every remarkable locality, this judgment shall be
publicly made known, to be kept in remembrance
for the future."

The sentence was duly executed in Rouen. The
notary Manchon produced a copy of the first trial,
out of which the XII. Articles were publicly torn

and burnt; and a cross was erected in the Old Market, on the place of the martyrdom. In Orleans the judgment was celebrated by a torchlight procession to the church of Saint-Sanxon, and the Bishop of Coutances and the grand inquisitor went to the city of the Maid themselves to promulgate it.

Isabelle d'Arc survived the restoration of her daughter's honour rather more than two years, and died at Orleans on the 28th of November 1458. Pierre des Lys, who had attained to the dignity of knighthood, and Jean, who was some time governor of Vaucouleurs, lived and died in honour, pensioned by the crown, and in the enjoyment of a small estate, granted to them by the Duke of Orleans, out of the great domain which their sister, Jeanne the Maid, had preserved to him.

When the services of expiation were performed in Rouen, Jeanne's hopes of her country were fulfilled. The English had lost everything but their old conquest of Calais, and the War of a Hundred Years was at an end. In January 1558, Calais itself was wrested from them, and they were then "*all thrust out of France except those who died there.*"

FINIS.

Ballantyne, Roberts, & Co., Printers, Edinburgh.